MY NAME IS NOT EASY

DEBBY DAHL EDWARDSON

SKYSCAPE

SKYSCAPE

Text copyright © 2011 by Debby Dahl Edwardson
All rights reserved

Amazon Publishing
Attn: Amazon Children's Publishing
P.O. Box 400818
Las Vegas, NV 89140
www.amazon.com/amazonchildrenspublishing

Library of Congress Cataloging-in-Publication Data

Edwardson, Debby Dahl.
My name is not easy / by Debby Dahl Edwardson. — 2nd ed.
p. cm.
Summary: Alaskans Luke, Chickie, Sonny, Donna, and Amiq relate their
experiences in the early 1960s when they are forced to attend a Catholic
boarding school where, despite different tribal affiliations, they come to
find a sort of family and home.
paperback ISBN 13: 9781477816295,   ISBN 10: 1477816291
1. Indians of North America—Alaska—Juvenile fiction. 2.
Alaska—History—1959—Juvenile fiction. [1. Indians of North
America—Alaska—Fiction. 2. Alaska—History—1959—Fiction. 3.
Interpersonal relations—Fiction. 4. Catholic schools—Fiction. 5. Boarding
schools—Fiction. 6. Schools—Fiction.] I. Title.

PZ7.E2657My 2011
[Fic]—dc22

2011002108

"Unchained Melody" lyrics by Hy Zaret, music by Alex North,
© 1955 (Renewed) FRANK MUSIC CORP. All Rights Reserved.
Reprinted by permission of Hal Leonard Corporation.

Book design by Alex Ferrari
Editor: Melanie Kroupa

Printed in the United States of America
Second edition

*For Saganna—George L. Edwardson,
who taught me to see the world through his eyes.
It's a good world.*

*"Oh, only for so short a while you have loaned us to each other.
Because we take form in your act of drawing us,
And we take life in your painting us,
And we breathe in your singing us.
But only for so short a while have you loaned us to each other."*
—Father's Aztec Prayer

Contents

1

PART I
The Day the Earth Turned Over
1960–1961

The elders say the earth has turned over seven times, pole to pole,
north to south.
Freezing and thawing, freezing and thawing,
flipping over and tearing apart.
Changing everything.

We were there.
We were always there.
They say no one survived the ice age but they're wrong.
There were seven ice ages and we survived.
We survived them all. . . .

My Name Is Not Easy
SEPTEMBER 5, 1960

LUKE

When I go off to Sacred Heart School, they're gonna call me Luke because my Iñupiaq name is too hard. Nobody has to tell me this. I already know. I already know because when teachers try say our real names, the sounds always get caught in their throats, sometimes, like crackers. That's how it was in kindergarten and in first, second, and third grade, and that's how it's going to be at boarding school, too. Teachers only know how to say easy names, like my brother Bunna's.

My name is not easy.

My name is hard like ocean ice grinding at the shore or wind pounding the tundra or sun so bright on the snow, it burns your eyes. My name is all of us huddled up here together, waiting to hear the sound of that plane that's going to take us away, me and my brothers. Nobody saying nothing about it. Everybody doing the same things they always do. Uncle Joe is cleaning his gun and Aaka—that's my grandma—is eating *maktak*. Jack is sprawled out on the bed reading *Life* magazine, and Mom's dipping water from the fifty-five-gallon water drum to make tea for Aapa, my grandpa.

Bunna's chasing Isaac across the floor on the opposite side of the room, showing him how to play cowboy with his authentic Roy Rogers gun and holster set. Pretending there's a whole pack of Indians under the bed. The only thing under the bed is one little Eskimo: our youngest brother, Isaac, mad about the fact he's always got to be the Indian.

I know that pretty soon Aapa's gonna finish his tea, and when he does, he's gonna belch and say *taiku*. But he isn't thanking Mom or Aaka or anyone, he's just saying it. *Taiku.* Thank you.

Some things are good to know, like knowing what lies on the other side of that smooth line the tundra makes at the edge of the sky. When you don't know, you feel uneasy about what you might find out there, which is how I'm feeling about Catholic school right now. Uneasy. Wondering if it's gonna be good or bad or both messed up together.

I never met them Catholics, yet, but I heard about them. *If you give them a kid 'til the age of seven, they got 'em for life.* That's what Catholics say. I watch Isaac scuttle across the floor, an uneasy feeling stirring in my stomach. Isaac is only six.

Aapa stands up from the table and belches good.

"*Taiku.*"

I wonder if Aapa knows what Catholics say. Probably not. Jack's the one who told us about them Catholics and he wouldn't say it to my *aapa* because Aapa is not a Catholic.

Jack is Mom's boyfriend.

Uncle Joe wipes his rag along the barrel of his gun and hands it to me, like he always does. "So. You going off to that place where they make you eat Trigger?" He leans down next to me when he says it, too, like he's sharing a secret.

I think about Roy Rogers' fancy horse, Trigger, in the movies they show at the community center sometimes, and I get an uneasy feeling in the pit of my stomach.

Joe smiles the kind of smile that says he knows stuff that other people don't know.

"You mean your momma never told you? Them Catholics, they eat horse meat."

Mom doesn't hear this because she's too busy pouring tea for Aaka. But Jack hears it, all right, and he's not happy about what he's hearing. I can see it in the way he looks up from his magazine real sharp, fixing his eye on Joe. Jack keeps his mouth shut, though, because Uncle Joe don't think much of white men, and Jack knows it.

"What they want to eat horse meat for?" I ask.

"Cheaper," Joe says.

Aaka is still eating *maktak*, and even though no one ever said it, I know them horse-eating, kid-stealing Catholics aren't ever going to feed me what I like—whale meat and *maktak*. And I'm all of a sudden so hungry, it seems like I could never get enough to fill me up.

Bunna flops down onto the bed next to Jack and Isaac. Jack's got a picture in *Life* magazine of a school somewhere down south in the Lower 48. It has one of those big orange school buses out front of it, and I don't like the way Bunna looks at that bus, his eyes all full of possibilities, because I know there's no way I am ever going to find any possibilities at all at Sacred Heart School, big orange bus or not.

Mom sets the teakettle on the stove, gazing at the three of us, her eyes soft.

"Isaac, your face," she says.

Isaac slips off the bed quick as a lemming, but Mom catches him quicker.

"You want them white people to think you're a puppy? Here, lemme wash your face."

I hear the plane overhead, flying low enough to shake the windows. I hold Joe's gun on my shoulder, sliding my cheek sideways along its smooth stock, trying to pretend it's not heavy, watching the plane buzz down out of the sky at the far end of town, like a big fat fly. It's one of them military planes, a C-46. I squint down the gun's barrel with my good eye as the plane lands, following it through the gun's sight as it drags its swelled-up belly across the tundra, sunlight flashing off its silver skin. The dogs are complaining about it, their voices yapping mad at first, then yowling up together into one voice, that long-tailed howl they always make when the plane lands.

As far as you can see out, there is tundra, tundra turned red and gold with fall, tundra full of cold air and sunshine. I take a deep breath. It feels like that plane has poked a hole in the sky, and all the air is leaking out.

I hand the gun back to Joe, the gun that's gonna be mine

when I'm old enough to take the kick. Next spring maybe.

"Boys?" Mom says. "You hear? Get your stuff. Plane's come."

I'm twelve years old, all right, and Bunna, he's ten. But Isaac, he's only six, and all I can think of is those Catholics and what they say about kids. Why can't we wait until Isaac turns seven?

When I climb up into that plane, the wind's blowing hard, same as always.

"Take care of your brothers," Mom calls, and I turn around quick. One last time.

The wind sweeps my hair across my eyes and carries Mom's words backward. It pulls me backward, too.

Stay here, the wind says. *Stay.*

Mom stands on the edge of the runway right next to Jack, my *aapa* and *aaka* and all our aunties and uncles with their babies. Some of our aunties are crying, but not Mom. Mom says we're Eskimo and Eskimos know how to survive. She says we have to learn things, things we can't learn here in the village. Mom does not cry, and neither do we.

Take care of your brothers. I hang on tight to those words as I sit down inside the plane. It's full of kids, this plane, kids going off to boarding school, mostly teens, because there's no high schools in none of our villages. Every single teen from every single village in the whole world, maybe—all of us being swept off to some place where there won't be no parents, no grandparents, no babies. Only big orange buses and trees and teachers choking on our names.

Bunna and Isaac are looking around with wide eyes.
"They all going to Sacred Heart?" Bunna whispers.

"Naw," I say. "Most of them going off to BIA schools."

Bureau of Indian Affairs schools don't take kids as young as us—that's what the man who convinced mom to send us said. He said we'd get a better education at a Catholic school. I don't say any of this to Bunna. I don't think Bunna cares much about his education right now. Me neither. And Isaac, sitting in between the two of us, doesn't even know what it means, yet, to get educated.

I gaze out the window at our family: a little knot on a fringe of tundra, waving in the wind. When she sees me, Mom opens her mouth and hollers. I can't hear her voice, but I can read my name on the shape of her lips, my real name. The name I'm leaving behind.

"How come we don't get to go BIA schools?" Bunna asks.

"Guess we're special," I say, and the kid sprawled out on the seat across the aisle grins big.

"You going to Sacred Heart?" he asks.

Bunna flops his head up and down.

"Hey. Put her there," the kid says, extending his hand. "Me, too."

And right then and there you know he owns Bunna.

"You ever been to Sacred Heart before?" Bunna asks.

"Sure," the kid says. "Sure have." Like he's been every-where and back again.

"So what's it like?"

"Well, it's not like home, all right, but you get used to it.

Know what I mean?"

We nod our heads, even Isaac, like we really do know.

Then I turn to watch out the window as the plane noses up into the sky. All the families get smaller and smaller, slipping away from us like peas off a plate.

"How far is it to Sacred Heart School?" Bunna asks.

"'Bout as far as the moon," the kid says.

Bunna looks out the window quick, his eyes big.

"I jokes," the kid says.

"What's your name?" I ask.

He leans over onto his elbow, like a cowboy in front of a campfire.

"Amiq," he says. He says it slow and sure, like he's daring the world to get it right.

Then the plane levels out and sweeps across the tundra, rising slowly up toward the sliver of moon that still hangs in the morning sky.

For a fraction of a second it feels like the earth below us has split wide open and swallowed up everything I ever knew. Like the earth itself is flipping over and falling away like it did a long time ago. Like there's a big scar down there on the tundra, a jagged place where the edges will never ever line up smooth again.

Not ever.

Looking for a Tree
SEPTEMBER 6, 1960

CHICKIE

I was five years old before I figured out I wasn't really Eskimo. It's weird it took me so long since I have hair as blond as snow, freckles like crazy, and a dad named Swede. I mean, who ever heard of an Eskimo with freckles, for Heaven's sake? But I never thought about this when I was a little girl in Kotzebue, Alaska, because Swede didn't have any use for mirrors, so our house never had one. They say I look like my momma, but I wouldn't know about that, either. Swede never had pictures. Now here I am at Sacred Heart School in a room with four beds, one huge mirror, and a picture of Mother Mary, big as life.

The one thing Swede told me about Sacred Heart was that I'd see a lot of trees here, and he was right about that—Sacred Heart School is in a valley that's full to the brim with trees. In the late afternoon sun, the ones outside my window shake their yellow leaves and wave their papery white trunks like dancers. Farther off in the distance are great big ones, dark as priests, poking holes in the sky with their prickly tops. This is all brand new to me because in Kotzebue, Alaska, there are no trees—not real ones anyhow.

Swede says the first time he ever saw my momma, that's where she was—high up in a tree. She was so far up, he didn't even see her at first, didn't even think to look up until he took his suspenders off to make a slingshot, and a couple of birds started laughing at him. That's what it sounded like, anyhow, because at the exact same moment my mother started laughing, two jays started screeching. When Swede finally looked up, there was my momma, sitting up in that tree like a big blond bird, laughing.

So all I ever wanted to do, just once, was to see what it would feel like to sit up in a tall tree, looking down, because my momma died before she could teach me about trees. I figure if you look hard enough in a place like this, you'll find a tree tall enough to reach the clouds—tall enough to reach Heaven, maybe, which is where my momma is, though Swede never says it. Aaka Mae—she's the one who helped raise me after Momma died—she says Heaven's a place way up in the sky where everyone is always happy and no one is ever sick and they eat pie every single day. Only you have to die to get there, which I, personally, have questions about. Someday I'll get answers, too, because I'm stubborn. When stubborn people have questions, they don't give up until they get answers. Stubborn people can probably figure out how to climb trees without anybody's help just fine, too.

At least that's what I figure, sneaking out the back door of the school when no one's looking. I'm going to find a tree to climb. A really tall one.

But right away I discover two really important things about the trees here at Sacred Heart School: most of them are either too skinny or too prickly to climb, and none of them have branches in the right places. If I want to climb a tree, I'm going to have to find one of those really big ones I saw from the window.

I think I'm heading in the right direction, but it's hard to tell because trees keep getting in the way, so I have to walk around them. Sometimes I find little trails to follow, but then the trails disappear, just like that, and it's nothing but trees again. The air has a sharp tang to it, too, like it's fixing to snow. And I'm getting cold.

When you see trees out a window, they seem sort of like people, each one with its own look, but when you're in the middle of them, they all look the same—an army of scabby trunks joined together with prickly arms, never ending. I can't even tell which way I came from now because no matter where I look, it's all the same. No way in, no way out.

I'm freezing.

All of a sudden I have a bad thought. A person could freeze to death out here and no one would ever find them. I stop walking and look around, trying hard to figure things out. That's when I realize that the sky filtering down through the trees is getting darker by the second.

I'm scared.

It feels like the trees are starting to close in on me. Pressing in so tight it gets hard to breathe. What am I going to do? What am I going to *do*?

I'm lost.

I start to run, desperate to get away, but the branches reach out and scratch my face, and the roots and rocks keep trying to trip me. When I stop to catch my breath, my heart is pounding against my chest so hard it hurts.

I want Swede!

I close my eyes tight and try to make him come. I know it's dumb, but it's all I can think to do. My feet are frozen to the ground, and I'm too scared to move.

That's when I remember something Swede said to Aaka Mae once: a person can always find a way out of a tight spot so long as they don't panic.

I take a deep breath, trying to ignore my stomach, which seems determined to panic.

Don't panic, Chickie Snow. Think.

I say this over and over and over until my body starts to relax.

Then I have an idea: If there's no way anyone's going to see me or even know where to look, I'm going to have to make noise. A lot of noise.

"Help!" I holler it as loud as I possibly can, but my voice comes out soft and squeaky.

"Help!" I try to make my voice hard and tough, but the cold wind gulps up the sound before it even leaves my mouth, and the dark swallows it. I start walking again, anyhow, hollering weak little noises into the bristly black shadows, feeling more hopeless every step I take.

I'm done for. Mother Mary, help!

Suddenly I see something familiar: a fifty-five-gallon oil drum lying on its side. I look around real good because it goes to figure that where there's oil drums, there's people. So now I'm standing here looking at that drum real hard, like it has to have the answer to my problem locked up inside it.

"Which way?" I whisper. "Which way?"

Everywhere I look seems full of black shadows. Then I get another idea. I pick up a piece of dead wood and start banging on the side of that drum, yelling like crazy.

"Help!" *Bang! Bang!* "Help!"

I keep at it, hollering and banging with such a passion, I don't hear anything else and don't even realize there's someone there until I see a fluttering of white emerge from the black trees like a ghost. And believe me, this is a sight that scares the sound right out of me.

Then I realize it's one of the nuns.

"Sister!" I bellow, running at her.

"My goodness," she says. "What in the world is going on here?"

She's really tall, tall as a tree, but something in her voice sounds more like a mother than like a nun.

"I . . . I got lost." My voice feels small, and there's a big, stinging lump of tears in my throat.

"What on earth are you doing out here?"

"Looking," I say, tears starting to roll down my checks. "Looking for a tree."

Sister sits down next to me, and before I know it, I'm crying for real.

"Looking for a tree," she says with a little laugh. "Well, it looks like you found one."

And all of a sudden, I start laughing, too, laughing and crying at the same time. Me sitting in the middle of an endless forest looking for a tree!

"You're not used to this kind of woods, are you?"

I shake my head.

"Me neither," she says. "We have bigger trees where I come from, but not so many. It's a bit intimidating, isn't it?"

I nod because even though I never heard that word before, I can tell what it means by the way she says it. Intimidating is the way these trees close in around a person, like they might try and choke you.

"It feels like this wilderness goes on forever," she says. I don't say anything because it seems like she's talking more to herself than to me. And anyhow, it feels good sitting right next to her, feeling warm and not having to worry about intimidating things.

"The garden is right over there," she says softly, pointing back the way she came. "See? You weren't really lost."

Off in the distance, I can hear the sound of a door banging shut and a hint of kids' voices.

"We just made a batch of cookies. Would you like one?"

I nod.

"What's your name, dear?"

I sure like the way she says that word—*dear.*

"Cecilia Snow," I tell her. "But people that know me always call me Chickie."

"Well, I'm Sister Mary Kate," she says, standing up, "and it's almost time for dinner, Chickie, so you and I had better hurry up inside."

And so we do.

Never Cry
SEPTEMBER 6, 1960

LUKE

Sacred Heart School is gray and shadowy, crouching in the trees like a big, blocky animal. I don't like the look of those trees, either, especially not in the dark. They're black and grasping, and they make strange flapping noises, like something mean's leaning over you, trying to suck the wind right out of you.

How could a person even breathe here? Back home, it doesn't get dark so early in the day this time of year, either, which make this place seem really wrong. Me and Bunna and Isaac are just standing here in front of the school, staring. This place doesn't look anything at all like those schools in *Life* magazine.

I can feel Mom's voice, whispering deep down inside— *Take care of your brothers*—and right now all I want to do is grab my brothers and run. Bunna is staring into the tree-filled darkness with wide eyes.

"You think there's evil spirits in there?" Bunna whispers,

watching the branches swing back and forth in the wind and ducking his head like he's afraid one might reach out and try grab him.

"Naw," I say. "There ain't." But I duck my head, too, for just a second.

When we look up, we both see him at the same time: a skinny, old priest. With his black clothes and clawlike hands, he looks like a big bald-headed raven.

"Bet that's where them preachers live," I whisper, nodding at those trees.

And suddenly that old guy looks really funny—both me and Bunna see it at the same time. Like he's pretending to be the kind of thing that would actually live in the middle of all those big black trees. The kind of thing that is scary and funny, both at the same time. Like at *puuqtaluk,* the costume contest back home, where old people dress up goofy to try and scare us and make us laugh, putting their parkas on inside out and dragging their arms across the floor like monsters learning to dance.

The priest's nose is mashed up weird against his cheek, too, like he's got a nylon stocking on his face, and now I see he's wearing a black *dress.* I look at Bunna and he looks at me, and we both start giggling. And every time we look at each other, we laugh harder. Just like at *puuqtaluk.* Even Isaac's laughing now, peeking out from under Bunna's arm.

I don't think Isaac even knows what's so funny. All he knows is we're laughing and sometimes, especially when you're scared, it's just good to laugh.

Then that old priest speaks. "How old is your brother?" he asks, looking right at Isaac, Isaac who isn't even seven yet.

It feels like everyone and everything has stopped breathing, even the trees.

"Six," Bunna squeaks before I can stop him.

"I see," says the priest.

I don't like the sound of those words, because the way he says it means that whatever it is he sees, it's something bad, something that makes him herd us into the school, away from the other kids, like we're sick or something.

"Sit over there," the priest says, waving at a bench by the wall. We sit, like rocks in the river, watching kids moving past us, staring. The priest swoops off into a room across the hall, and a door shuts behind him with a snap. We sit on a hard bench, waiting. It feels like we wait forever. Finally, an old lady in a long white dress opens the door, and the priest sweeps past her without a word, throwing shadows up and down the hall.

"Your little brother is too young for Sacred Heart School," the lady tells us. "They shouldn't have sent him." Her voice sounds soft and weak, like a scrawny seagull way up high. But her hand reaching for Isaac's shoulder is hard as a steel trap. "There's a family in town where he can stay for a while, until we get things sorted out."

They're stealing Isaac.

My heart starts to beat so fast, I'm sure I'm gonna choke.

"It's only temporary," she says.

They're taking Isaac away. Forever. That's what she's really saying. I can feel it. But I don't speak. My throat is frozen.

Another lady bursts out of the office, waving a piece of paper. This lady is big and solid and wears a skirt and sweater the color of ashes.

The old lady looks at her. "Father's gone to get the station wagon," she says.

Father's gone to get the trap. That's what she really means.

"Here's the affidavit, Sister," the lady in gray says, handing the paper to the old lady.

I watch the way Sister holds that paper, reading it slowly, and I think about that word, *affidavit.* It's a word I never heard before.

"It's a permission form, Mildred, not an affidavit," Sister says sharply, reading it slowly, like she's looking for something. Something bad. "*In loco parentis,*" she says. "Good."

"Father will need to have it notarized," Mildred says, looking up. "Oh look, he's already got the car."

Sister looks out the window, and I do, too, still chewing on that stringy word: *notarized.* It sounds like something that might hurt. Outside a long square car pulls up in front of the school.

"Come along then, Isaac," Sister says, pulling Isaac by the shoulder. Me and Bunna start to follow, but she turns to look back at us, still clutching Isaac. "You two, go with the other students," she says.

We look back, but the others are gone. The hallway is empty and dark and full of nothing but whispery echoes and dark shadows. Sister looks back, too, then nods. "All right then, gentlemen. You two may follow. I'll get you settled *after*."

After feels like a big black hole, and Sister is perched on the edge of it, clutching Isaac. Isaac's eyes are spots of bright black terror.

What am I going to do?

We follow Sister outside, where the one she calls Father— the one with the squashed face—is sitting in that car, waiting. And before I even get a chance to move or call out, "NO!" Father reaches out, pulls Isaac inside the car, and Sister slams the door, stepping back, her white dress flapping in the night.

He's got our baby brother; that priest has Isaac.

Isaac is trying to pull away from him, all right, but he's too little. And I'm trying to run after him, but that old nun is clutching *me* now, her skinny fingers sharp as steel.

"That's enough," she says. "He'll be fine."

Her voice sounds just like a seagull, a seagull circling above someone's meat rack, getting ready to steal.

We watch as the car drives off, Isaac's face pressed up against the window, his eyes pleading, me standing there. Helpless.

What am I going to tell Mom? What the heck am I ever going to tell our mom? I was supposed to take care of my brothers.

Bunna and I follow Sister, like she says, the two of us pressed together tight—a broken fist of brothers. She takes us to the place where there's food and leaves us, still clinging together, at the tail end of the food line. We're too scared to eat right now but too hungry not to.

I can still see Isaac's tear-streaked face pressed against the window of that car. Like it's happening over and over, like time's folded in on itself, and part of me is always going to be trapped on this side of things, watching that car disappear into the dark woods with my little brother trapped inside.

Gone.

I'm starving, all right, but all I know right now is that hunger feels the same as fear, sitting in my stomach, hard.

They call the place where us kids are supposed to eat a cafeteria. It's big and square with long tables and steaming food and it's got two sides: the Indian side and the Eskimo side.

"What about Isaac?" Bunna whispers. "Where's Isaac gonna eat?"

"He's okay," I lie. "They gonna feed him better food where he's at."

Like I know.

The nun with the meat is tall enough to be one of the *inukpasuks*, one of the big people, but I don't say this to Bunna.

"Don't touch the meat," I whisper.

Bunna is really hungry, but he's scared enough to pull his tray back quick when I whisper it. I'm not sure what made me say it—I just don't trust this place, not even the meat. Especially not the meat. Who knows where it comes from?

"No meat?" the *inukpasuk* says. Her face looks confused, and even though she's very big, I see right away that her face is more of a girl's face, the kind of girl who is someone's friend.

"Are you boys sick? Maybe I ought to take you to the infirmary? Have you caught the flu?"

"We never," I say.

Bunna nods quick. "We never."

I don't know that word *infirmary* and I don't like the sound of it, either. *Infirmary.* Like someplace where you get put into, maybe. Like a cage or a net or a long square trap.

The giant nun looks at the other nun—the old one with the seagull voice—and it seems like she's waiting to be told what to do. That's when Amiq steps up behind us, grinning. I don't guess that kid ever quits grinning.

"Sister Mary Kate, these boys are members of the Whale Clan. They can't eat this kinda meat right here." His voice is smooth as water.

Whale Clan? I don't know what the heck a Whale Clan is, and by the look on her face, I'm guessing Sister doesn't know either. But Amiq just smiles right up at her like she's his favorite aunt or something.

"They can't eat this kind." He leans up real close to the nuns. "You know. *Taboo.*" He whispers that word like he's telling her a secret.

"Oh. Well. I see," Sister says quickly. And blushes. Then she looks at Bunna's tray.

"Why, you didn't even get any milk!" she says. "Milk's good for you, boys. You will drink some, won't you?"

Sister sounds so worried about it that I raise my eyebrows quick to say "yes." I don't tell her we don't like milk, especially not Bunna. Milk always makes our stomachs hurt, sometimes.

Especially Bunna's.

"Yes?" she says anxiously.

"Sure, Sister," Amiq says. "Lots of milk."

When I catch Amiq's eye, I have to look away quick because all of a sudden I don't have any control over my feelings. I might start crying or I might start laughing, and I can't tell which. Everything feels weird and scary and funny, all mixed up together: us not eating meat and that old nun piling my plate sky high with string beans and carrots, and the way she watches Amiq out of the side of her eye like he's a dog about to make a mess.

When she hands him his plate, Amiq looks at his food and says, "Why thank you, Sister!" smiling from ear to ear like string beans and greasy carrots is the best kind of present a kid could ever get. And all of a sudden I have to stare really hard at all those beans to keep from laughing, because if I start laughing now, it's going to hurt. If I start laughing now, I'm probably gonna die laughing. Sometimes laughing is the worst kind of crying there is.

"Now you know how to take care of them nuns," Amiq whispers as we walk away. He nods back at the tall nun and winks at the old one, his grin as sweet as cake.

Winks!

And for half a second it looks like that old bird might even be trying to smile back.

That Amiq, he's something else.

"What's a Whale Can?" Bunna asks.

"Clan," says Amiq. "That's *Indian talk.*" He nods over

at the table where the Indian kids sit, staring at us. "This is Indian country, so we gotta talk that way sometimes. It's what them nuns understand."

"But how come you said we can't eat meat?" Bunna asks, switching into Iñupiaq. He looks first at Amiq and then at me. "That's a lie. We could eat meat anytime we want."

Amiq looks at me for a second and says, "It's not a lie," smiling.

You can tell Bunna's trying to figure this out. Amiq looks like he's trying to figure it out, too. "You know how they have to keep ocean foods separate from land foods, right?" he says suddenly.

Bunna nods. Everybody knows how in the ice cellar you have to store whale meat and caribou meat in separate rooms. That's true.

"You know what happens if you don't keep them separate?"

Bunna frowns. He doesn't know.

"You die," Amiq says.

Bunna snorts, like he thinks it's a joke, but you can tell by his eyes that he isn't quite sure. "Yeah, so how we gonna know how they store their meat?" he says.

"That's right," Amiq says, quick as anything. "How we gonna know?"

I fill up my glass with milk, watching the nuns out of the side of my eye. Bunna fills his glass real slow. He's watching the nuns, too, especially that big one, the *iñukpasuk*.

"They gonna make us drink all of it?" he asks.

The milk looks lumpy.

"*Atchuu*," I say, shrugging. "It won't hurt you."

"Why can't we just get meat instead?" he asks. "Them guys know how to keep meat, I bet."

"Don't matter how they keep their meat, okay? We still don't eat it."

Bunna scowls.

"*Horse meat!*" I hiss. "They're trying to make us eat *horse meat*. Okay?"

I'm talking in Iñupiaq and saying it hard, but as soon as the word leaves my mouth, I wish I never said it, because Bunna's mouth gets real small, like a little zero, and you could tell he's thinking about Roy Rogers and his horse, Trigger, who is someone a person would never want to eat. I know I should tell him it's just a joke, but for some reason I just don't want him touching that meat.

"I want to go home," Bunna whispers.

"Me, too," I say, loud and sharp. "And we will. Soon."

"Is it horse milk, too?"

"Of course not," I say. As if I know.

We sit down at the table, still talking, and I can feel them Indians watching, which is why I'm talking louder than usual and talking in Iñupiaq, too. I want them to wonder about what I'm saying and I want them to know by the sound of my voice not to mess with me. I'm concentrating so hard I don't even notice that old priest, the one that took Isaac, hovering over top of us, tapping a ruler against the side of his hand like he's keeping count of something. Tapping the whole room quiet until pretty soon it feels like everybody is holding their breath, watching us.

"And what was your name again, young man?" the priest says. The way he says it is like he's saying something else. Something bad.

"Luke," I say.

Amiq, behind him, mouths the word "FATHER," then looks down quick.

"Father," I add quickly.

"Put your hands on the table, Luke," Father says.

I do what he says, and he slaps the backs of my fingers with his ruler, slaps them hard enough to make the sting run up and down the sides of my arm like lightning.

"Here we speak English," he says.

I stare off into the cafeteria, my face blank. *I will not cry . . . I will not cry.*

"Yes, Father," I say, looking down like I'm supposed to.

I will never cry.

Then, before Father can say another word, Bunna grabs his milk and drinks the whole glass fast, lumps and all, gasping for air like his life depends on it.

Indian Country
SEPTEMBER 6, 1960

SONNY AND CHICKIE

Sonny was here last year and so was Amiq. They both knew the rules. This side of the cafeteria is Indian Country and that one over there is for Eskimos. Two sides, just like a board game—just like that chess game one of the volunteers had taught them how to play last year. The floor even looked like a chessboard, with big black and white squares. On this side of the board, Sonny was king. The other side was Amiq's.

Everyone else knew the rules, too, everyone except those two girls, sitting at their own table in their own field of squares: one black-haired and one blond. Those two were out of the game altogether. Or maybe they'd already been captured, Sonny thought, watching the way the dark one's long hair rippled across the side of her face. Her name was Donna and she'd been here last year, too. She never said a word to anyone about anything.

Skittish as a wolf.

Last year she always did the same thing: held her cafeteria tray in front of her chest like it might protect her, trying to find the safest spot to sit. Sometimes she found a spot off in the corner, away from everyone, where she would sit real quiet. Sometimes she wouldn't even eat. Sonny paid attention to these kinds of things because he was used to looking after kids. That's how it is when you're the oldest kid in a big family.

The freckled white girl with her was new and younger and, unlike Donna, she was so full of words she didn't seem to have any control over when they came out or what they said. And you could tell that it didn't make a bit of difference to her where *she* sat. Her name was Chickie, and she and Donna were roommates. Sonny'd heard her talking to Sister Mary Kate.

Sonny hadn't seen that other kid until just now—he was small and unnoticeable, wearing huge black-framed Alaska Native Health Service glasses and sitting at the far end of the girls' table, all alone—a little Eskimo with bad eyes. Sonny hadn't noticed him until he shoved those glasses up onto the bridge of his nose, shifting himself into Sonny's field of vision with that one little movement.

Suddenly two more new girls were steering their trays across the room toward Sonny, sliding down onto the bench next to him like they'd known him forever, which they hadn't. Sonny, in fact, had never before seen either one of them. But even though they weren't from his village, they were Athabascan, just like him, and they'd figured out the lay of the land in one shot. He moved over to make room for them.

The one girl was named Rose and the other was Evelyn.

Evelyn reminded Sonny of old Anna Sam back home. Tough as a wolverine, with the kind of eyes that never missed a thing. And right now she had her eyes trained on Amiq, who was marching across the cafeteria with his little string of Eskimo pawns. Evelyn didn't like the looks of Amiq, you could tell, but she'd already figured out how things worked here at Sacred Heart School, and she knew that Amiq was the one Eskimo you had to deal with if you were going to deal with Eskimos.

"Somebody oughtta teach that kid a thing or two," she muttered, looking straight at Sonny, like she figured Sonny'd be the one to do the teaching. Sonny nodded.

The nuns had given them plates full of stringy meat, mushy vegetables, and perfectly rounded scoops of potatoes with brown gravy poured on top, which made them look like ice cream sundaes, the kind you could buy at Dairy Queen in Fairbanks if you were rich. The meat was okay, but the potatoes had no taste at all. The gravy didn't taste right, either. Like someone had drained all the fat off.

"Swede never lets us eat fake potatoes," Chickie announced loud enough for the whole place to hear. She wrinkled her nose for emphasis.

Donna didn't say anything and neither did any of the others. Rose and Evelyn watched Chickie suspiciously from the sides of their eyes, and the Eskimos gave each other looks.

Chickie put her chin up high, looked right at Sonny, then grinned at all the Eskimos, even at the little one sitting off by himself.

Fearless, Sonny thought. *Dumb, but fearless. Where the heck did she come from?*

"Hey, Junior. Come sit by us," she called out, and the little kid with the big glasses picked up his tray, obediently, and moved over, shoving his glasses onto the bridge of his nose again and glancing around, like he was embarrassed to be singled out, embarrassed to move and embarrassed not to. All the Eskimo kids nodded at him and smiled like they all shared some private joke.

This made Sonny nervous.

You don't quiet down, them Eskimos gonna catch you when you go outside to pee and chop your head right off. Play kickball with it. That's what Sonny's mom used to tell them when they got too wild back home. And when you're a little kid needing to pee and it's dark outside, talk like that can scare the pee right out of you.

But when you're a big kid at Sacred Heart School and you know your grandfather and his brothers used to kill Eskimo trespassers . . . well, that kind of talk just makes you tough. And Sonny was plenty tough.

Now, Amiq was marching his Eskimo pawns right past Sonny's table—on the Indian side—acting like he owned the place. Evelyn glared. "Who say they gonna be here?" she muttered.

Amiq stopped dead in his tracks and turned around real slow. "*We* say," he said, staring right at Evelyn. And smiling a great big smart-aleck smile. Like he was laughing at her.

Evelyn's eyes got black as water under river ice. You didn't have to know her to see she was not the kind of girl who let people laugh at her. "Yeah? So whatchu *doin'* here?" she snapped.

Amiq just stood there, grinning down at her.

"Scouting," he said, like he was some kind of cowboy or something.

That word made Sonny's chest tighten. *Scouting.*

If there's gonna be any kickball around here, Sonny thought, *it's not gonna be my head.*

Amiq sauntered over to the heart of the Eskimo table, grinning down at Chickie as he passed and winking at Donna.

To Sonny's surprise, Donna blushed.

Chickie shoved another forkful of gluey fake potatoes into her mouth. All of a sudden she was missing Swede really bad. When Swede had told her about going away to boarding school, he never said anything about fake potatoes, that's for sure. The only thing he said was that she was going to a place called Sacred Heart School and she couldn't bring her hula hoop. He'd looked right square at the hoop and said it, too: "You can't take it with you, Chickie. Sorry, girl."

But that was okay by Chickie because you can't go anywhere on a hula hoop and Chickie had known forever that the one thing she wanted to do in life was to see what it's like to live in a place where the roads don't quit rolling at the end of town.

That hula hoop had been the only hula hoop north of

the Arctic Circle, too. It had come north to Kotzebue on the barge, which is how Swede always ordered stuff for the store. Which is why Chickie always got to eat real potatoes instead of fake ones.

"Real potatoes taste a whole lot better than fake ones," Chickie announced.

"I don't care for potatoes," Donna said quietly.

Chickie put her fork down with a sigh and studied the dry brown meat, slimy vegetables, and wedge of pie. At least the pie looked good. She took a bite of it, just to see, watching the nuns, who still stood by their food in the food line. It was apple pie with real apples and it did taste good.

Apple pie is as American as Wheaties and milk. That's what Swede said one time. Not that they ever got Wheaties and milk at home. They'd probably get lots of Wheaties at Sacred Heart, though, lots of Wheaties with this lumpy powdered milk. Canned milk was better. Why couldn't they have canned milk? Chickie took another bite of pie and looked at Donna sideways.

"I wonder if that tall nun is the one who does the baking," she said. In fact she was pretty sure that the tall one, Sister Mary Kate, was the pie baker, but she figured she ought to be polite, her being new and all. Aaka Mae said she had a tendency to be bossy, and she wanted to be sure not to be too bossy with her new roommate, her first friend at Sacred Heart School.

The nuns were starting to put the food away now, and Donna had turned to watch them. Chickie turned, too. An old priest was standing next to the wall by the door, all draped in black. He looked like a black cat, that's what Chickie thought. Like a big black cat waiting to catch something live in his skinny old claws. Donna looked at him, too, but only for a second. Then she looked away quick like she already knew that priest, already knew all about him.

Chickie looked back at the nuns, but she could still feel that priest watching them. It made her skin prickle. She quickly took another bite of pie, studying the way the nuns were putting away the food.

"The tall one is Sister Mary Kate," Chickie told Donna, helping herself to more pie. "I wonder if she's going to teach us how to cook. She's a good cook, don't you think?"

"Maybe it's the other one who makes the pies," Donna said.

Chickie almost laughed out loud. She didn't want to be rude or anything, but that skinny old nun disappearing into the kitchen with stringy beans looked way too mean to make a pie this sweet.

Chickie looked back at the priest, but he wasn't looking at her and Donna, she realized suddenly. He was watching the boys. Boys take a lot more watching than girls do. That's what Chickie figured.

"Did your mom teach you how to cook?" Chickie asked Donna.

She tried to say it real easy like a normal kid would say it, a kid with a mom. But Donna gave her a funny look anyhow, like she knew.

"I never learned to cook," Donna said quietly.

It's true that a person can tell things about another person without anybody saying it. For instance, you can almost always tell by their hair which girls have mothers and which don't. Chickie's hair was wild as a snowstorm, whereas Donna's was tame as black syrup. Chickie teased a piece of pie crust back and forth across her plate, suddenly self-conscious.

"I don't have a mother," Donna said.

Chickie looked up, surprised. Donna took a bite of her own pie and didn't say another word.

Two of the Eskimo kids were talking to each other in Eskimo, and Chickie could see right away that the priest did not like this. Not at all.

It's true that some people get mad when they can't understand what other people are saying, and Chickie could tell that this priest was one of those kinds of people. She looked back at Donna, but Donna wasn't looking at the priest and she wasn't looking at Chickie, either. She was looking straight out the window, her eyes empty, like she'd gone someplace else, someplace where priests couldn't go.

Chickie looked out the window, too. The moonlight was shining on the yellow-leaved birch trees outside, making them twinkle and dance in the wind. For a fraction of a second, it got so quiet, Chickie swore she could even hear the sound those leaves were making.

Sonny felt a sudden chill in the air and looked around. Most of the other kids were still busy shoveling their mouths full of food, hungry after a long day of missing home. Those two

Eskimo brothers were talking together in their own language. Sonny watched them closely, trying to figure out what they were talking about.

"Horse meat!" the bigger one muttered, unaccountably. *Horse meat.* An English word nobody ever used, laced into an Iñupiaq sentence. Weird.

Before Sonny even had a chance to figure it out, the whole room went dead quiet, and everyone looked up, as if by instinct. That old priest was striding toward the Eskimo table, black as a storm cloud, shaking the whole place into an electric silence. He stopped right next to those two brothers and towered over them, tapping his hand with a ruler.

Some of the other kids might have wondered why he needed a ruler at dinnertime, but Sonny already knew, and so did Amiq. The two of them eyed each other without meaning to.

Checkmate, Sonny thought, watching Father and ducking his head. Even without looking he could feel Father, standing there like a big black bishop in a game of his own—a bigger, meaner game.

And then the only sound in the whole room was the sound that ruler made, smacking that kid's hand. Hard.

Sonny still didn't look. No one looked. They all sat there leaning into each other, one body of kids with a whole lot of dark, averted eyes.

That Amiq should have warned his kids about Father, Sonny thought, glancing sideways at Amiq. *He should have told them.*

How Hunters Survive

SEPTEMBER 7, 1960

LUKE

It's still dark outside, like this is the kind of place that's always gonna be dark. And I can't sleep.

All I can hear is the sound of other boys breathing. I think maybe I hear the whole place breathing—every last one of them. Nuns and priests, girls and Indians, all of them fast asleep. Bunna looks tense, even in his sleep, clutching Isaac's toy gun. He didn't think I noticed that he had it, but I did. Some of the younger kids are making little hiccupping noises, hunched into their blankets, trying not to let anyone hear them crying.

I wonder if Isaac's asleep now, too, wherever they took him. I try real hard to imagine him sleeping—snoring soft with that twitchy little sleep smile he gets. But no matter how hard I try, all I can see is his tear-streaked face, pressed up against the black window of that car, disappearing into tree-shaped shadows.

I stare up at the ceiling, wishing a person could go from

one place to another, just like that. I'd make myself go from this lonely bed at Sacred Heart School to my own bed back home, curled up with my brothers—both of them.

I have never in my whole life been spanked, and I'm wondering what's so bad about Iñupiaq that they have to make your hand sting for speaking it. I can still feel those Iñupiaq words, warming the back of my throat, only now it feels like the sounds got twisted around somehow. Like if I try say a word, it's gonna come out bent.

But I know for sure what I gotta do now. I lean over the side of the bunk and shake Bunna hard.

"Bunna. Wake up. It's time," I say real soft.

"Time for what?" he asks, his voice loud and groggy.

"Shhh. Time to go home."

"Where's our stuff?" He's wide awake now, whispering.

"We don't need stuff."

"I'm taking Isaac's gun," he says, his voice rising a bit. Isaac's toy gun is on the bed, next to him. He slept with it, I just realized.

"Go ahead," I say. "Take it."

Outside it's dark, but there's a moon slung low, and the dirt road that leads away from the school is lit with a shadowy light. It's the same road that priest drove down when he took Isaac away, his car spitting stones and dust. At the end of that road is the highway that leads north to Fairbanks and south to Anchorage. If we can find Isaac and hitchhike north to Fairbanks—and then get a message to Uncle Joe somehow—we can get home. Uncle Joe has a friend who flies planes.

"I'm hungry," Bunna says. "We oughtta eat first."

"Eat what? Horse soup?"

This shuts him up.

We're coming up on the place where the school road turns out onto the highway. There's a cabin on the corner there and it has its lights on.

"Wait here," I tell Bunna, but he don't listen. He follows right behind me like a shadow.

"What the heck you doing?" he asks.

"We gotta find Isaac. Maybe this is where they're keeping him. Stay low."

We sneak up to the window of that cabin and peek in. Part of me already knows we aren't going to find our brother in there. The other part is desperate enough to look anywhere.

Inside is an old Indian man sitting there, all alone, wearing dirty brown coveralls, staring at his stove and drinking coffee. He's got his back to us, and the hair on the back of his head looks matted, like he just woke up. He looks mean, even from behind. When he stands up, I duck down quick, my heart pounding. Now what?

I think about my grandpa's uncles, killing all them Indians, but I don't feel that brave. All I feel is a sudden need to get off that road and out of sight.

"We gotta cut through the woods behind," I whisper.

Bunna looks at those big old black trees, moving their branches back and forth like fingers. "What about Isaac?" he says in a small voice.

"I don't know where they got him. We gotta go get Uncle Joe to help us."

Bunna is still looking at the trees. "I'm not going in there," he says.

I don't want to go in there either. "You rather stay here? That what you decide?"

"No," Bunna whispers. "I never."

"Okay then."

Bunna and I never been in woods before, and right away we don't like it. There's things on the ground you can't hardly see: roots and rocks and bushes and pieces of tree. Things that make it hard to walk. And the trees lean in so close that when you look up, you can't even see the sky.

This place is not right. You're supposed to be able to see things when you're outside. You're supposed to be able to look out across the tundra and see caribou, flickering way off in the sunlight, geese flying low next to the horizon, the edge of the sky running around you like the rim of a bowl. Everything wide open and full of possibility. How can you even tell where you're going in a place like this? How can you see the weather far enough to tell what's coming?

Bunna trips, and there's a sudden pounding sound that makes my heart stop cold, makes me grab him hard.

"It's only birds," Bunna says firmly. Like he's trying to convince himself.

"Whatcha trying to do, get us killed?"

"It's only birds, Luke," he repeats, but his voice doesn't sound all that sure.

"Yeah, well, you gotta be more careful."

That's when we hear the crack of something way bigger than birds, something crashing through the woods behind us and veering off through the bushes in front: a big bull caribou.

"*Tuttu*," Bunna breathes, and we both relax. This place feels better now, with caribou in it.

"And us without a real gun," I say.

"Yeah," says Bunna,. "We coulda had real meat."

I'm not sure what we would have done with a dead caribou, us trying to run away, but I don't say this to Bunna.

We look off toward where that *tuttu* went, and we can see light up that way, like the woods is letting go. Without a word we both start running and suddenly there it is: a big, wide-open chunk of tundra, right in the middle of the woods. We race out onto it, laughing and shoving at each other and falling onto our backs, staring straight up into the star-spangled sky where the pink of dawn is just starting to spread. We breathe deep. The whole sky breathes with us.

"Feels almost like home," Bunna says. "You think we can make it, really?"

I guess he's thinking about that long bus ride we took getting here and that longer plane ride.

"Yeah, sure. People hitchhike. We just gotta get onto the highway," I say, trying to pretend it's that easy, not wanting Bunna to know the truth: I can't figure out where the road's at. Hard to tell anything in the middle of all these trees.

Bunna sees him same time I do—that mean old Indian, standing there at the edge of the tundra, holding a gun. We both jump, dumb as ptarmigan. He must have seen us, must have followed. He walks toward us real slow. Hunting.

"What you doin' out here?" His voice is raspy.

"Going home," Bunna says before I can stop him.

The old man's frown lifts just a bit. "You kids from the school?" he asks.

"Were," Bunna says.

"We're headed home," I add quick, giving Bunna a look.

"Road's that way," old man says, tilting his head as he runs his fingers over the barrel of his gun. Bunna and I shift, uncomfortable.

"You boys making too damn much noise. Scarin' the animals."

When he moves toward us with that gun, we know we're done for, and both of us jump up and start running like our bodies are connected by one single muscle, a runaway muscle. We run out across the tundra and off through the black woods, leaping over fallen trees and rocks and bushes without even looking back, not once.

The tree branches try to grab us, all right, but we don't stop until we trip, both of us tumbling together into a dark, black, empty space. It's like a room, this space, a room made out of trees. The trees surround us like they're trying to protect us, and suddenly we feel safe, lying on our bellies in the silvery darkness. We can hear that old Indian walking carefully through the woods, like he isn't quite sure which way we disappeared. We hold our breath as the sound gets closer and closer and then starts fading away until all we hear is the sound of water. We sit up, grinning. On one side of us, a little finger of light filters through the trees. We stick our heads out. It's a lip of land that overhangs a river, and across the river the sun is rising. The smell of water gives us energy, makes us feel like we can make it anywhere. We can get Isaac and escape those giant nuns and mean priests and their fog-gray school. I know we can.

We find the road, all right, but it seems like it goes on forever, winding through trees and hills and more trees. Bunna's started to complain again, and if I weren't the oldest, I'd be complaining, too. Feels like this road is one big hill with no top and no bottom. We're winding up the side of it, and there's a straight wall of rock on one side and—suddenly—nothing on the other. When I look down, my breath gets sucked right out of me. Bunna's eyes are wide as eggs.

"Holy cow," he breathes.

Down below us, the side of the road drops off into a deep valley, lined with trees. The trees look soft from up here, like tundra grass, billowing in the morning breeze like low-lying clouds. A rocky river rushes along the valley floor, shining silver green in the morning light. Looking way far down at that river makes you feel strong and dizzy, both at the same time. But you can still smell the water, even this far up you can smell it, sharp as gunmetal.

"Wow," I whisper.

At first we don't even hear the sound of the car behind us, but when we finally do, it don't matter. The only place to go is down, straight down, which would take wings. We're trapped.

It's a priest, driving that long, skinny car. The same car that took Isaac away—same priest, too, I bet. He's driving slow, like he's hunting.

"Shoot," I say, looking down the mountainside.

Shoot. Breathing it out quick, like a bullet.

They got us now.

The priest pulls up alongside us, but it's a different priest, a younger one. He pushes the car door wide open and leans over across the seat, chatting like there's nothing strange about two Eskimo kids trapped on the side of a road in the middle of Indian country. His eyes are empty, blue like the sky. I never seen eyes like that before.

"Enjoying a little walk, boys?" he says.

Bunna nods fast, like guilty people do. The priest smiles.

"Nice day for it," he says, patting the seat next to him. Bunna hops right in without a second thought.

"Only one problem"—now he's frowning—"you boys missed breakfast, and now you're about to miss class as well."

Bunna glances back at me like a trapped animal. I slide into the car next to him and ease the door shut, trying not to look at that priest and his ice-blue eyes.

"I'm sure you just lost track of the time," he says.

Bunna lets out a small sigh of relief and nods.

We sit there while the car winds its way back down the road, none of us saying a thing. We don't know how to talk to priests, and this one is humming like it don't much matter if we even talk or not. I stare out the window, watching the trees whip past us like a wall of green and black stone.

"You boys are from the North, aren't you?" he says, finally, tapping the steering wheel with one finger.

Neither of us says a word. Bunna looks at him and raises his eyebrows real quick. *Yes. We're from the North,* his eyebrows say.

I frown.

"And I bet you're both seasoned hunters."

Now he's looking directly at me, his eyes like chips of pale blue ice.

I turn away, staring at the wall of trees. "Yes," I say, soft as leaves.

"Good," he says, his finger still tapping the steering wheel. "You see, the way this works is Sacred Heart School is run largely through volunteer effort." He peers down at Bunna. Suddenly all I want to do is pull Bunna away fast and say, "*Listen: we're not even Catholic.*"

But I don't.

"Do you know what *volunteer* means?" the priest asks.

Bunna shakes his head. I stare out the window.

The priest's boney white hand grips that steering wheel, one finger still tapping—a long, sharp pointer finger.

"Well, it's like this," he says. "The Lord gives each of us talents—each special skills—and he expects us each to use them for others. That's what we're doing here—volunteering our talents for the sake of the school. It's our way of giving back to God what he has given to us."

He frowns down into the valley. "Now, me, I'm not much

of a hunter, but I do know a thing or two about carpentry. And Father Mullen—you and your brothers met him last night, I believe? Well, he's a boxer. Would've gone professional if he hadn't been promised to the priesthood."

I think of that old priest with the mashed-up face and feel the sting of his ruler running up my arm. So our brother Isaac was kidnapped by a boxer. A boxer priest. I look over at Bunna, nervous, but Bunna is not thinking about these things. I can tell.

"And old Sister Sarah, why she can make anything grow—even up here in the frozen north land," the priest continues.

"What about the other one?" Bunna says.

The priest looks down at Bunna, surprised.

"The other one?" he says.

Bunna rolls his eyes upward. His eyes say *iñukpasuk* loud and clear, so clear even the priest understands.

"Oh," he laughs. "The tall one—that's Sister Mary Kate."

Bunna looks up, curious, like he really really wants to know about Sister Mary Kate's special talent.

"Well, let me see. Sister Mary Kate is very"—he taps the wheel—"she's so very eager and so very . . . ah, big," he says. "And I'm sure that must be useful, don't you think?"

He's still smiling. I swallow a smile, too.

"So what about the hunting?" I ask, surprised to hear myself talking so easy all of a sudden.

"Ah. I was just coming to that. You see the thing is, we want to eat, now, don't we?"

Bunna nods.

"Well, so that's where the hunting comes in. Everything we get here comes through donation or hard work. We need you boys to work for us by hunting."

Bunna looks down at his lap. He's still holding that dumb toy gun, fingering it nervously, like he's forgotten he has it.

"Do you hunt horses?" he says, his voice doubtful.

The priest looks puzzled. "Hunt horses?"

Then he looks down at Bunna's gun. Bunna shoves it into his pocket, embarrassed, but it's too late. The priest is laughing.

"Ah, yes. I had forgotten. Cowboys, eh?"

Bunna scowls. He don't like to be laughed at.

"Well, I'm sorry, boys, but we haven't any horses."

He pats the steering wheel like it's a dog.

"Guess we'll just have to make do with this old buggy."

Then he leans down toward Bunna like he's sharing a big secret. "And you know, I don't think cowboys hunt horses as a rule. Think about it. How would they get around if they started eating all their horses?"

Bunna glares at me real quick.

"Yeah," he says. "How would they?"

We drive on in silence, the priest smiling and still tapping the steering wheel real soft, like maybe it helps him think to tap it that way.

"So you're the Aaluk boys," he says at last.

The way he says it is like he already knows, so we don't say anything.

"And which one are you?" he asks Bunna.

"Bunna," Bunna says.

Then he looks at me. "And?"

"Luke," Bunna says.

"You're the oldest, aren't you?" Still looking at me.

I raise my eyebrows. *Yes.*

"Well, there's no point in trying to run off, you know. It's about 300 miles to Fairbanks, and I doubt you boys could make it that far. And besides, if you try this again, Father Mullen will be the one to come after you." He gives us a look. "And believe me, Father Mullen cannot abide a runaway."

Abide is one of those church words. I'm not quite sure what it means, and I don't want to find out, either.

"You'd rather help us hunt, now, wouldn't you?"

I nod. My mouth is suddenly dry as dust.

"All right then, here's the deal: You don't run away anymore. Instead you work hard in school and earn your way by hunting. That's easy enough now, Luke, isn't it?"

I nod, and he smiles. He thinks he's solved everything, thinks everything is easy all of a sudden. He doesn't know about my name, my Iñupiaq name. My real name is not Luke and it's not easy, not at all. But I could hunt; he's got that right.

I'm a hunter, and hunters know how to survive.

Snowbird

OCTOBER 1960

CHICKIE

All four beds in my dorm room have girls assigned to them. We never knew each other's names until we got put together in this room. There's Donna, who's Yupik, sitting stone still on the bed across from mine, like she's in church or something. And on the top bunks are two other girls named Rose and Evelyn. Rose and Evelyn are Athabascan, and from the way they act, you might think they knew each other before they got here, but they didn't. Evelyn is from Northway, and Rose is from Nenanna.

Rose and Evelyn are chatting away, but Donna just sits there, like she's waiting for someone to give her permission. She always wears this necklace with a big old gold coin on the end of it, and when she gets nervous, she takes hold of that coin and rubs it with her thumb real soft, like she hardly knows what she's doing. Like maybe it's magic or something.

Evelyn has put a towel over the mirror on our dresser. She

MY NAME IS NOT EASY

says it's spooky and I say she's right because before she put that towel there, I kept seeing people out of the corner of my eye. And when I'd turn to look, I'd realize that it was just that darn mirror, following my every move like something creepy.

I have decided that I definitely do not like mirrors.

Evelyn says her grandpa is the traditional chief of Northway, and Rose says her grandma is like a chief because she tells everyone what to do and everyone listens. I tell them that Aaka Mae makes the best bread in Kotzebue, but she is not bossy. I also tell them that Aaka Mae never runs out of flour because Swede owns the store.

"Who's Swede?" Evelyn asks.

"That's my dad," I say.

"Why do you call your dad 'Swede'?" Evelyn says.

I give Donna a look. "That's his name."

"What do you call your mom?" Rose says.

I glare at both of them. "I don't have a mom," I say. "She died when I was born."

Everyone gets real quiet.

"My mom left when I was five," Donna says.

She's talking so soft, we almost have to quit breathing to hear her. And she's looking right at me.

Left? Forever? That's worse than having your mom die.

"Her name was Sister Ann," Donna offers.

"Your mom was a nun?" Evelyn says.

I glare at Evelyn for the rude way she says it, but secretly, I really want to know, too. How could Donna's mom be a nun?

"My parents died from measles. I was raised at Holy Cross

Mission by Sister Ann. Before she got called to serve some-where else."

Rose and Evelyn shift on their bunk, uncomfortable. Truth is, none of us knows what to say.

"When I was a baby, I thought she was my mother," Donna says.

From the way she says it, warming her hand on that gold coin necklace of hers, I'm guessing she still thinks it. I stare at her necklace and swallow hard. "What kind of money is that?" I blurt it out without meaning to.

Donna looks at me, surprised, then looks down at her necklace like she just discovered it.

"It's not money. It's a Saint Christopher medal. He's the patron saint of travelers," Donna says. "Sister gave it to me the day she left."

Seems odd to give someone a traveler's medal when you're the one leaving, I think. But I don't say it.

"Did you live with her?" Rose asks.

"Yes," Donna says.

"Did you sleep in the same bed with her?"

Donna gives Rose a funny look. "No."

"Do nuns sleep in beds?" Evelyn asks.

I'm wondering about this, too, but when I look at Donna, she has such a lonely look on her face that I say, "Of course they do," right away, glaring at Evelyn.

"I wonder if they even have hair," Evelyn says.

"Well, obviously," I say. Watching Donna.

"How would you know?" Evelyn challenges.

I have to admit, she's got me there. How would I know?

"You think you have to be bald to be a nun?"

"Yeah, but how would you know which ones have hair and which don't?"

"Easy."

"Oh yeah?"

"Sure."

"Prove it."

"What do you want me to do, pull out a piece of their hair?" As soon as I say it, I'm sorry.

"Yeah," Evelyn says. "A piece of hair. A piece of the tall one's hair."

Never let your opponent smell fear. That's what Swede always says. I keep my face as blank as snow.

"Easy," I say again.

"Bet she doesn't have any hair at all," Rose says.

"Bet she does," I say.

Bet it's the same color as mine, too, I think, but I do not say it.

The nuns are all at chapel, and we're supposed to be in bed. I find Sister Mary Kate's room in one shot because her name is on the door. It's not even locked. This is going to be easy.

Sister's room is small, with no bunk bed. It has a bedside table just like ours. There are four things on that table: a book that says DIARY on the front, another book that says *The Collected Poems of Emily Dickinson*, a Bible, of course, and a funny-looking comb with a long, pointy handle. I pick up the comb, and sure enough, there's one strand of hair on it, one strand you can barely see, because Sister Mary Kate's hair is blond as sunlight, just like mine.

I smile. I know I should go right back to our dorm room, but I am a curious person, and I don't give up that easily. Swede says curiosity killed the cat, but I am smarter than the cat. I pick up the diary and open it to the first page.

Sister's diary is filled with a cursive handwriting that is very pretty, but skinny and kind of hard to read. I have to squint to make it out, like someone who needs glasses.

> The children looked so small and needy sitting before me like a sea of dark faces. It would be hard to tell the difference between the Indians and Eskimos, except for the fact that they seem to segregate themselves into two groups.

I stop reading, surprised. Hard to tell the difference between Indians and Eskimos? Maybe *Sister* needs glasses.

> Father Mullen told us that this animosity is due to savage feuds. It will be our job to teach them to behave as educated Christians, our job to teach them that they must be the ones to eradicate the rampant ignorance and poverty that exists amongst their people.

I do not know what to think about this. What do these words mean? *Animosity, savage, eradicate, rampant, ignorance, and poverty.* We do not use these kinds of words in Kotzebue.

"Well?" says Evelyn.

We're sitting at breakfast, watching Sister Mary Kate, and now all four of us—me, Donna, Evelyn, and Rose—know that Sister Mary Kate has hair, and we all know it's the same color as mine. Only longer. But Evelyn wants to know more.

"So what else she got?" Evelyn says. "How come you never say?"

She leans close to me when she talks because the boys are sitting right next to us and we both have agreed, without actually saying it, that Sister's stuff is none of their business.

"Well?"

I look over at Sister Mary Kate, and she looks back like she knows we're talking about her. My cheeks get hot, and I suddenly feel very, very guilty.

"She doesn't have anything. Just a comb and a Bible and a book of poems written by some lady." My cheeks get even hotter and the boys are starting to look at me, too. Me and my red freckles.

"Hey, Snowbird! How come you get so red?" says Bunna. Bunna started calling me Snowbird because my name is Chickie and I am white like a snowbird. He thinks he's funny. Now all the boys next to him are chirping "snowbird, snowbird," like a winter chorus of big wild birds.

I wish I could melt right into my chair, but instead I sit up straight and stare right at my opponent, just like Swede says to do. *Look 'em in the eyes*, Swede always says, which I do.

"My *aaka* says you aren't supposed to *mess* with snow-birds." I spit the words right at Bunna, and his eyes get wide. *Bingo*. Bunna still has a smirk on his face, but he isn't laughing anymore. I bet you money his *aaka* has told him that if you are mean to snowbirds, you will never be a good hunter. That's what Aaka Mae always tells boys.

"Come on, girls," Evelyn says, glaring at Bunna. "Too many Eskimos here. Let's go." She heads for the door.

Evelyn is trying to make me feel better, but this only makes me feel worse. This world doesn't have too many Eskimos. It has too many sides and too many closed doors and too many people who don't understand.

That's what I think.

Kickball
SPRING 1961

SONNY

Sonny watched as kids fluttered up the hall on their way to lunch like a thick flock of ravens. Junior, Chickie, and Donna were laughing at some joke.

Those two Eskimo brothers—Luke and Bunna—were stuck together behind Amiq like an Amiq-shaped shadow. And Amiq, as usual, was looking for trouble.

"So you been out hunting lately?" he was saying, saying it real loud, too, like he wanted to make sure everybody heard him. Like he wanted to make sure Sonny, in particular, heard him.

Sonny did. He knew those brothers. They were always out in the woods. Hiding from Indians for the most part, he figured. Not hunting.

The older brother, Luke, looked at Amiq like he wasn't sure what the heck he was talking about. Then he glanced back at Sonny with a nervous look. Sonny scowled.

"Yeah. Hunting. Me and Bunna," Luke said—like he

knew he was supposed to say it but wasn't sure why. You could tell he was trying to sound tough.

Sonny wasn't fooled.

Amiq was still eyeing him. Like he was daring him to do something.

"You ever run into that old *Indian*?" Amiq said. He used the word *Indian* like an arrow aimed right at Sonny. Rose and Evelyn and the Pete boys sidled up next to Sonny.

Luke frowned, as if he were trying to remember something. Or maybe forget it. "Yeah," he said.

"And he said to quit scaring off all the animals, right?" Amiq coached.

"Yeah! He did!" This was the younger brother, Bunna. "And he acts like he's gonna shoot us, too, but he never."

Suddenly Amiq burst out laughing, like it was a really funny joke. Possibly the funniest joke in the history of funny jokes. The sound of that laugh made Sonny stop walking and turn to look back at them, hard. *That little smart mouth.*

Now all of them had stopped walking and they were all watching Sonny and Amiq.

"Heck, that old guy ain't gonna shoot nothing," Amiq said. "He's half blind, that one."

Only he didn't say blind, he said "*plind.*" And he looked right at Sonny when he said it, too, like he was accusing *all* Indians of being half blind.

"Plind," Sonny mimicked.

Evelyn giggled. "How come he talks like that?" she whispered.

"He's from Barrow," Sonny said loudly. "I mean *Parrow*. That's how they *dalk*."

Rose and Evelyn giggled.

"That old Indian's probably waiting for somebody to scare the animals his way so he could eat sometime," Amiq told Bunna, glaring at Rose and Evelyn. "He's so blind, he can't even find his own butt in broad daylight."

The muscles in Sonny's jaw tightened. He could level that guy, one shot, if he wanted to. Level them *all*. He glared at the one closest to him—nervous little Junior with the big glasses. Junior backed away, shoving those glasses up onto the bridge of his nose.

"What's he eat then, he don't catch nothing?" Bunna was saying.

"Rotten fish," Amiq said, watching Sonny sideways.

Bunna held his nose like someone'd farted. "*Aqhaaa!*"

That was it. Sonny reached out, grabbed Bunna by the collar and held on tight, twisting his hand a little. Bunna scowled like he was trying to look tough. Or at least trying to look a little bit brave.

Now they were in the middle of a big pack of kids. Kids pressed in on either side of them like two walls: the Indian wall and the Eskimo wall. The Eskimo wall had one blond head, that little white girl they'd nicknamed Snowbird. The Indian wall looked hard as rock with no breaks in it, not even a crack. Sonny smiled.

"Better than raw meat," he said. He knew about how Eskimos ate their meat frozen. Frozen and raw.

The older brother, Luke, pushed his way forward through the crush of kids. Amiq was right behind him.

"Leave him alone," Luke growled.

Sonny shook Bunna, just for good measure, and let go of him. He wasn't about to fight some little kid.

Amiq shoved himself forward. "Back off," he snapped, muttering "half-a-gas-can" under his breath. And he aimed those words right at Sonny, too. "*Pack off.*"

Sonny laughed. "Make me," he said.

"Why'd he say half-a-gas-can?" Snowbird whispered.

Nobody said anything. Everyone was staring at Sonny and Amiq, who stood in the middle of the crowd, glaring at each other. Then Sonny turned toward Snowbird.

"'Cause he don't know how to say 'Athabascan,'" Sonny said. "He has trouble *dalking.*"

Amiq clenched his fists. "Go ahead," he sneered, looking up at Sonny. "Go ahead."

The whole pack pressed in closer, both sides taunting.

"Punch him! Punch him!"

"Do it!"

Sonny reared up and smashed down on Amiq with a force hard enough to make him fall back into the crowd. But before Sonny could even step closer, Amiq had sprung up, tearing into Sonny like a wolverine. The kid was smaller, all right, but he was tough, Sonny thought. Plenty tough.

"Go for the throat!" someone hollered. "The throat!"

Now everybody was yelling, everyone except that one Yupik girl with the long black hair and little Junior, who stood off to one side, nervously fidgeting with his glasses.

Suddenly a door flew open and Father Flanagan came racing down the hall, his robes billowing out like black sails.

"Break it up, boys! Break it up!"

"Shaving cream," Junior whispered, cursing like his grandma taught him.

Father shoved himself between Amiq and Sonny, forcing them apart. The two of them strained against his hold like dogs at the ends of their lines. But Father's arms were strong and sinewy.

"All right, boys, that's enough. That's quite enough," he said.

He let go of them, finally, and they pulled away, wiping their faces and glaring at each other sideways. The crowd pressed itself flat against the sides of the hall, tried to melt into the wall—one thick body with dozens of eyes, watching. No one said a word.

"All right everybody, break it up," Father said. "It's lunchtime now. Get going."

But before they could even fan out, he laid his hands on Amiq's and Sonny's shoulders.

"Not you two," he said, reeling them in with his voice. "You two have earned yourselves a little conversation with Father Mullen."

"Aw, Father, c'mon," Amiq said. "We were just *playing.*"

He put a barb in the word for Sonny's benefit. Sonny glared at him, then looked away.

"Yes, and Father Mullen is not very fond of games, I'm afraid. Let's go," the priest said.

As they walked off, behind Father Flanagan Sonny could hear the others, whispering among themselves.

"Oh man, that Father Mullen, he's mean," Bunna said. "He might kill Amiq."

"It wasn't his fault, was it?" Chickie said. "He was just protecting himself. There's no sin in that, is there?"

"Depending on how you look at it, pretty much everything's a sin," Junior said.

Father Flanagan sailed off down the hall with Sonny and Amiq trailing behind him like two fish on a stringer, trapped in the wake of a big black boat.

Father Mullen's office was dim and musty smelling, and Father Mullen's eyes were just plain crazy. Sonny couldn't really say what it was that made them crazy, but whatever it was, it was right there, just under the surface, like a big fish in dark water. Amiq saw it, too, Sonny could tell. You'd have to be blind not to.

Sonny saw, as well, the worn two-by-four in the corner of the room, which he was trying not to look at. He and Amiq stood together. Waiting.

White people don't know how to be comfortable with silence the way Indians do. Sonny knew this. Without even thinking about it, he understood the difference. When Indians don't talk, it's because they don't need to, because things are already understood, and everybody knows it. When a white guy like Father Mullen doesn't talk, it means something else altogether. Father Mullen's silence stalked them from the edge of the room like a shadowy animal.

"The fight's in your blood, isn't it?" he said finally.

His voice made Sonny squirm. He saw Amiq twitch.

"Do you understand that you can be expelled for this sort of behavior?"

"Yes, Father," Sonny said as fast as he could.

"Yes, Father," Amiq echoed.

"Mr. George"—Sonny's skin crawled at the way he said his name. In Father's mouth the word *Mr.* sounded small and ugly—"do you suppose your mother saved up to send you here just so you could learn to scuffle like a ruffian with your fellow students?"

"No, Father."

"And Mr. Amundson"—he turned to Amiq—"do you suppose those scientists who sponsored your education did so for the purpose of training you in the science of *cat* fighting?" He spat out the word *cat* so hard, they could feel its claws.

Sonny glanced sideways at Amiq, but Amiq was looking down at his feet. Sonny looked down, too. He didn't know how *Mr.* Amundson was feeling, but he, Sonny Boy George, was mad about the way Father Mullen had dragged his mom into the room. He stared at his feet hard, remembering how his mom had stayed up late at night threading those tiny beads by the smoky light of the kerosene lamp, making slippers. He studied his shoes, his brand-new shoes, thinking about all the beadwork his mom had to make in order to pay for those shoes. In order to get him here.

The air in Father Mullen's office was close and stale.

"I said, 'the fight's in your blood, isn't it?'" Father hissed.

"Yes, Father . . . I mean no, Father," Sonny mumbled.

"No, Father," Amiq added.

"'Yes, Father. No, Father.' You boys seem to be suffering from some confusion." His voice was tight and terrifying. Like a gun about to fire.

"Yes, Father, No Father." They were both saying it now, no longer sure about who was saying what.

"Confusion," Father snapped, "is the mark of the *Devil*." His eyes were shining with a strange light, and they both backed away, instinctively, both of them suddenly aware of that two-by-four waiting in the corner behind them.

"And let me tell you something, gentlemen. In this school there's only one kind of fighting allowed."

Father's voice was ominously low, but Sonny looked up, surprised. *Fighting allowed?*

"Boxing," Father said, his voice like a fast punch. "Do you know what that is?"

Sonny nodded. Amiq raised his eyebrows.

"You wear gloves, follow rules, and when the fight is over, you shake hands. That's the only kind of fighting we'll tolerate here. Anything else, and you'll be punished. Severely. Keep it up, and you're out. Do. You. Understand?"

"Yes, Father."

"Yes, Father."

Both of them were nodding together, like two heads on one neck, both of them eyeing the door for deliverance. Father dismissed them with a curt nod.

Then, right there at the door, just as they were ready to step across the border into freedom, that crazy Eskimo—Amiq—he raised up one fist, held it tight against his chest, and grinned. *Right at Sonny.* Maybe he thought Father didn't see him, but he was wrong. Father sees everything.

Before they could even move, Father flew to the corner and grabbed the two-by-four. Sonny felt the force of it cracking against Amiq's bones as if against his own. But Amiq just stood there, his back bent to Father's blows, staring at the door to freedom, smiling.

Amiq and Father were both in their own narrow spaces, both seeing only what they wanted to see, but Sonny saw it all—the bent back, the crazy priest, the smile stretched so tight across Amiq's face, you could probably snap it like slingshot rubber—and something else, something in Amiq's eyes—a look no two-by-four could ever touch. And even though Father couldn't see it from where he stood, you could tell by the way he was swinging that paddle that he knew it was there.

Sonny watched Father, imagining what it would feel like to slam a kickball right through Father's gut, right out that door, right down the hall, reverberating from floor to ceiling like gunshot.

Indian kickball.

And when he played it, he would win.

The Size of Things Back Home
SUMMER 1961

LUKE

It seems like everything in the world has changed. Then we get home and it seems like nothing has changed. Except for the size of things—the door has gotten shorter and the window, lower. Mom seems smaller, too, somehow. Small and brittle, like she might break. She watched us getting off the plane and kept watching. Even after we had walked all across the runway, she kept watching, holding her heart and waiting for Isaac, knowing, just like we knew, that he wasn't there. Isaac's gone. It had to do with papers we didn't understand. And now, none of Mom's letters to Isaac—the ones she sends to the school—get answered. Mom moves about the house and no matter what she's doing, it still feels like she's holding her hand over her heart, missing Isaac. But she won't talk about it. Whatever there is to be said about Isaac, nobody's saying it. Not to us kids, anyhow.

The hurt of Isaac's absence slaps back and forth between us like a closed curtain over an open window. Aaka eyes it sometimes, then looks at Mom, but Mom doesn't look back. She just sighs and keeps on making their tea.

Aapa sits his Bible on the washstand in the corner, right alongside his typewriter, just like he always used to. And that's where he stands, pecking the Good Word into Iñupiaq with his two old pointer fingers, letter by letter. Same as ever.

Me and Bunna are sitting by the door, waiting for Uncle Joe, and I am looking out across the room, remembering how it used to be when we were little—not so long ago, when I think about it. But it feels like forever.

We used to play cowboys and Indians here. Isaac was always the captive Indian—exploding out from underneath the bed, clawing his way across the plywood floor like a blind lemming and getting caught every time. I remember him bumping right into Aapa, once, making Aapa's fingers slip from the typewriter keys. Making him type wrong.

The words that came out of Aapa's mouth that time were not good ones, not in any language. He reared up like a bear, raising his big old arm, ready to swat us. But before he could finish his swing, Aaka had her broom out, and Aapa stopped in midair, dropping his arm and bending his back with a little smile, like he was just waiting for Aaka to hit him. And she did, too—Aaka, hardly any bigger than us boys—she hit that broom so hard against Appa's back, it cracked the handle right in half.

It makes me smile, too, when I remember Aaka, waving her splintered broom in the air, spitting mad, scolding Aapa like an angry squirrel.

Aapa pulled his parka from the hook that time and shuffled out the door without looking back, his voice soft as rain. "You boys ever gonna learn?" He came back later, holding out a brand-new broom for Aaka like a stiff bouquet, smiling.

I sit here, nodding at the memory: Yes, we learned. We learned how not to talk in Iñupiaq and how to eat strange food and watch, helpless, while they took our brother away.

There's a clatter of sound as an empty coffee cup rolls across the floor. Mom sighs and mutters, "Clumsy." Then she scurries across the room to retrieve it.

Mom isn't talking to any of us, really, but when her eyes meet mine, there are tears there, tears that make her eyes look like they've turned to water.

"Why can't we just go find him?" I whisper.

Mom looks at me, her eyes full of hurt and something else, something that makes me feel protective, suddenly, like I'm the parent and she's just a little kid.

SONNY

Old Anna is gone now—that's the only thing I know, reading Ma's letter, all alone at Sacred Heart School after most of the others have left for home.

Nobody here knew a thing about Anna, who died in her sleep, all alone.

Old Anna and her canned peas. That's what she and I used to eat back home when I used to chop wood for her. Canned sweet peas. We ate them together, after the wood was piled, the two of us sitting at her table, a can of sweet peas between us. I sure miss the sound of that spruce wood crackling in the barrel stove on a day when it's so cold outside, the river ice cracks like gunshot. Us two enjoying the smooth taste of those peas and the smell of smoke, firelight flickering on the walls.

Best candy there ever was, those peas. Anna kept them hidden in a case beneath her bed, and I was the only one she ever shared them with. And she'd always talk with me while we ate them, too, the rasp of her voice mixing with the crackle of the fire, like they were both part of the same thing.

"Your mom still sell slippers to white people?" That's what she asked last time I saw her.

I nodded. Yeah, Mom was still selling her slippers.

Anna nodded, too, but I could tell she wasn't thinking about white people or even slippers so much as she was agreeing with the way Ma did things. Maybe she was even a little bit surprised at how Ma went to Fairbanks and came back practically the next day with sugar and flour and new clothes for all us kids, never even stopping off at the bars on Two Street like most folks did.

People always pay a lot for beaded Indian slippers, and Ma's are the best, with big blue and red beaded flowers on the toes, worked in a way that made them look more interesting than some people's. That's how she got the money to send me to Sacred Heart School, too.

"Because you're gonna be a leader someday." That's what Ma said.

Old Anna never said it, but there was something in the way she nodded her head that time that let me know she agreed with Ma. I was gonna be a leader.

But now old Anna's gone, and I'm all alone feeling like I didn't do something I was supposed to do. Something important. Something I'll never ever get to do again.

CHICKIE

I step off the plane and for a second I just stand there, sucking it all in: the smell of ocean and tundra and the sweep of sky. It's funny what you miss about a place. I missed seeing the ocean ice out there on the horizon, holding the wide-open world in place like a fence.

I don't know the guy meeting the plane, and he doesn't know me, either. From one of the villages, I figure.

"Where you going? Teachers' place?" he asks.

I guess he thinks I'm one of the teachers' kids.

"No. The store."

He looks at me funny, like he can't figure out why a white girl would fly all the way up here just to go to Swede's dusty old store.

"Swede's my dad," I say.

He looks puzzled for a second, then smiles. "I'll be darned."

If I were smart-alecky, like Amiq, I'd say, "What the heck's that supposed to mean?" But I'm not. And anyhow, I already know what it means. It means he doesn't think of Swede as having a family, especially not a young one.

"You could climb up into that truck, and I'll run you over there," he says. He's looking at my freckles and trying to pretend he's not. Measuring my freckles against Swede's, probably. "Could see Swede in you all right," he says.

I lift my chin and look right at him. "How's Aaka Mae?"

He knows who Aaka Mae is—everybody knows Mae and everyone calls her Aaka, too, like she is the whole world's grandma, which she pretty much is.

"Aaka Mae? They take her to Fairbanks."

Fairbanks? It gets hard to breathe all of a sudden. I watch wordlessly while he heaves my suitcase into the back of his truck. Clouds of dust rise up behind us as the truck bumps along the dirt road, taking us to Swede's store. All I can think is: *Aaka Mae, gone.*

LUKE

The door swings open, and there's Uncle Joe, holding his gun and grinning. The sun shining behind his head looks like a halo or something.

"So they gonna let you hunt down there?" he says.

Me and Bunna are suddenly tongue-tied staring at that gun, the one that never ever misses a shot.

"Sure," I manage finally. "One moose or three caribou— that's one semester's worth."

I don't think Joe knows anything about semesters or tuition and I don't think he cares, either. But I can tell by the way he looks down at his gun that he's calculating moose and caribou to bullets.

Then he looks up—looks right at me, hard. "You take care of your brother, now, okay?"

I nod, looking at the gun, calculating the best way to angle the barrel, shooting through trees.

CHICKIE

Standing in the store, I suddenly realize that for some totally crazy reason, I actually missed the smell of Swede's store, with its fox furs on the wall and cans of stove oil on the floor and its dusty shelves full of flour and jam and coffee and nails. There's two ladies in the back of the store, one young and one old, debating about which fabric to buy, and this makes me realize, suddenly, that I missed hearing the sound of Iñupiaq, too.

And I especially missed the feel of Swede, crushing me up against his flannel shirt without a word. We don't need a lot of words, Swede and I, because that's how we are. We always know what each other is going to say before we say it, so a lot of times we don't even bother talking. Swede already knew about my first question, for example. I can see it in his eyes when I pull away from his hug and look at his face.

He looks down, folding his arms across his chest like he's trying to hug himself.

"They had to put her in a home."

The way he says *home* makes it sound like it's some new word, a word that has sharp, hissing edges and doesn't have anything at all to do with family.

"Why?"

For a moment that word just sort of hangs there in the air between us like a hook.

"She needed to be there," Swede says.

One of the ladies plops a bolt of fabric on the counter and says, "Three yards." Then she turns back to the older woman and asks, in Iñupiaq, if that's going to be enough.

I stand there watching Swede measure the material, thinking about how the English language makes me so mad sometimes. *She needed to be there.* How can a person use the word *needed* in a sentence that has nothing whatsoever to do with need?

LUKE

Bunna and I are standing by our duffles, all ready to go. It's not like the first time we left, that's for sure. I'm thinking about all the kids I'm going to see—Amiq and Donna and Junior. I miss them all—even the Pete boys. Even Sonny, which surprises me. We are watching the plane land, and I'm already thinking about soaring back up into those summer clouds and landing in the middle of all those trees. I even miss the trees.

I'm holding Uncle Joe's gun with Bunna right next to me like a sergeant at arms. Mom is standing off to the side, looking lonely. Jack's gone now, has been for months. No one's sure where he went, and none of us miss him much, either, except for Mom. I put my arm around her, looking down at the gun, proud of myself. I want her to be proud, too, but Mom's not looking at the gun; she's looking first at Bunna, then at me, then back to Bunna, like she's trying to memorize our faces, trying to keep herself from crying by looking extra hard. And then Uncle Joe is here, striding cross the tarmac and smiling big as day.

"Hey!"

He nods at the gun one last time. "I'm only loaning her to you, remember. Don't you forget to bring her back."

I hold the gun up, smiling as hard as a person can smile.

"I won't," I say.

"Yeah?" Joe winks, which makes his whole face wrinkle up like tissue and makes me notice, for the first time, all those little wisps of gray hair around his ears.

All of a sudden I want to say no—no, don't get gray hairs, no, don't let us get on this plane, no, don't let us leave with this gun of yours.

But before I know it, I'm sitting in the seat by the window, listening to the rising roar of the engine and watching everything get smaller—and smaller—and smaller.

CHICKIE

When we land in Fairbanks, all I can think about is the word *home*, the home where Aaka Mae is at—somewhere here in

Fairbanks. Where exactly is it and what's it like? The home I am imagining is a very lonely place. I look around and spot the little knot of Sacred Heart students congregating in the corner of the airport. Like orphans. Watching them, I have a sad thought: I'm halfway to being an orphan myself, Swede getting older and all.

How come I always have to think like this? I try to make my mind go somewhere else by imagining myself way up high, looking down at this fidgeting little fistful of kids, standing together at the Fairbanks airport, the boys making jokes and the girls ignoring them. Then I have another one of those thoughts: Maybe someday all of us will be like Aaka Mae, sitting in homes that are not really homes. All alone and forgotten.

Suddenly, Evelyn hollers out my name, and I run to her like I'm running to meet a long-lost sister.

PART II
The Day the Soldiers Came
1961–1962

We are living underground and we are many.
I can't see the others but I can feel the warmth of their bodies and
feel their hunger, too.
Their hunger is my hunger.
Up on the surface, there is meat, frozen meat.
We know this.
"Is it warm enough to go up?" they ask.
"Too cold," I say.
We all know the danger of cold and so we sleep,
dreaming our collective dream.
Sleep until the time comes.
Sleep.

Rose Hips and Chamomile

SEPTEMBER 1961

DONNA

We work in the garden, Sister Sarah and I, silent as stones. In the quiet between us, you can hear the things you can't hear when people are talking and making noise. Like birds way up high, calling back and forth to each other, and the soft sound of wind tapping against the birch trees. Yellow leaves float down around us like feathers.

Sister stands to move from one part of the garden to another. Her habit flickers in the light, casting shadows where she walks, and I think of myself, always living within the shadow and light of the nuns.

The first one was Sister Ann. I really didn't understand that she wasn't my real mother. It was winter, cold enough to freeze our blankets to the wall, and all anyone ever said was, *her time to leave the Mission has come.*

I thought I was going to leave with her, but I was wrong.

I watched her dash out across the runway, her white habit

slapping in the wind, the wind that is always with us. Slapping back and forth across her legs, telling her to stay.

She pressed something cold and flat into my hand, and I stood there clutching it for dear life, watching her leave without me. Because I knew right then, without anybody having to say it, that I couldn't run after her, couldn't even say how much I wanted to.

She had tears in her eyes, too. This is what I saw. Tears that made her eyes look shiny when she turned to look back at me—me, standing still and dumb on the edge of the tundra, unwilling to believe the truth of what my eyes were seeing.

I watched her step right up into the belly of that metal bird, watched the plane lift off toward Heaven, watched it fade into the roaring sky, my momma with it. Gone forever. Because I knew, even then, it was forever.

And I didn't make a single sound, either, because little as I was, I knew I was supposed to hide my feelings. I don't remember ever not knowing this.

The last thing Sister Ann told me was to have faith, because everything happens for a reason. I didn't understand what she meant then and I didn't know anything at all about reasons, but I believed her. I have always believed her. And I still remember the words of the prayer she taught me: "Guard well Thy inner door where we reveal our need of Thee." I am always guarding my inner door, keeping people away.

It was a Saint Christopher medal she'd given me and it had the year engraved across the back of it, like a secret message: 1953. I rub my thumb against those numbers now for comfort. Comfort is round and cold and hidden, pressed hard against my chest out here in the chill of Sacred Heart garden, where Sister Sarah and I are working, side by side, without a word.

I don't know why Sister Sarah picked me to help in the garden. Every single girl but me raised her hand. I really wanted to work in the garden, but I knew she wouldn't pick me. The others raised their hands because they were afraid not to. Sister Sarah has a ruler, just like Father Mullen, and I've seen her slap kids' hands, too, just like Father. But she isn't mean like he is. She doesn't have any anger crouched up inside her like Father does, only sternness. And she treats everyone sternly, even herself. I like this about her.

It's time to dig up the last of the potatoes. That's what Sister says, showing me how to follow the plant stem to its roots and the roots to the potatoes. She doesn't talk and I don't, either. She digs, and I watch how her fingers read the roots. Then I do it, too.

Sister looks almost like she's praying, kneeling in the garden, digging potatoes. And when I think about it, it does seem like a way of praying, pressing our knees against the cold, black earth.

"See how the plant hides its potato?" Sister says, and I nod.

Guard well Thy inner door where we reveal our need of Thee.

Sister told the others she picked me because I know how to sit quietly. But out here on the edge of the woods, where you can see snow-covered mountains above the dark trees, she says something different: She picked me because she knows I have a green thumb. She doesn't explain what a green thumb is or how she knows I have one, but I think I already know. Having a green thumb means you can feel the whisper of green things, deep down inside you, like a special kind of prayer.

Tiny flecks of snow are falling from the sky. They flicker against the trees like little chips of light, and you can tell it's going to snow hard some day soon. But right now it's more like play, like the snow and the sky are teasing each other.

Part of me wishes we could stay out here forever, but the other part knows this won't happen, of course, and that part isn't even surprised when Sister Mary Kate bursts into the garden, squawking like a giant bird and swirling the falling snow into nervous flurries.

"Sister! Sister! They've found a moose. Dead. On the highway."

Sister Sarah brushes every last bit of dirt from the potato she's just picked, moving very slowly, like she never even heard Sister Mary Kate.

"I imagine these things happen," she says at last.

For some reason this makes me smile. I am not quite sure why Sister saying it's normal for a moose to die on the highway should make me smile, but it does. I dig deeper into the cold ground, following the spidery roots, looking for another potato, trying to pretend I'm not really listening. But I can't help thinking about that moose on the highway, the highway that threads up the sides of the mountain and disappears into the clouds. I am wishing as hard as I can that I could run right up into those cloud-wrapped mountains, where I've never been before.

Salvaging meat sounds like a frightening thing, the way Sister explains it. She looks at me helplessly, like she wants me to dig something out of the ground that will excuse her from salvaging, but all I can think of is how badly I want to go up onto that highway and see that moose.

"Well, surely it's an act of Providence," Sister Sarah says calmly. "We need the meat now."

Sister Mary Kate tilts her head sideways, thinking. "Why, yes," she says slowly. "It *is* an act of Providence, isn't it?"

Sister Sarah lays a potato in her basket and then carefully reaches down to run her fingers over the tops of the tiny yellow flowers that grow on the edges of the potato garden.

"Chamomile," she says. "Makes a tea that calms the spirit. Did you know that, Donna?"

I shake my head.

"It's a useful thing to remember," she says, and I nod.

Sister Mary Kate remains standing above us, one hand worrying the other, waiting for Sister Sarah to say something else, but Sister is too busy to notice. She's laying stems of chamomile into her basket in neat rows of tiny fluffy yellow heads.

"Oh, Sister!" Mary Kate cries suddenly, "I've never in my life butchered an animal! I mean I wouldn't even hurt a fly, I just hate to see them suffer, don't you know? But Father

Mullen has put me in charge of this poor beast and . . . oh, dear! What am I going to do?"

Sister Sarah stands up slowly, clutching her basket of potatoes and flowers.

"Preparing meat is no different than gardening. This is how we sustain ourselves," she says. "It's all part of God's plan, Sister. If you work in that spirit, it becomes simple."

Sister Mary Kate puts her hand to her heart, looks skyward, and sighs with relief.

"Oh, thank goodness!" she says, reaching out to help Sister Sarah with her basket. "I knew you would know what to do. Will you come show us then?"

Sister Sarah smiles a very small smile. "Show you? What in the world would I show you? I haven't the faintest idea how to butcher a moose."

Sister Mary Kate's face crumples, and at the exact same moment I hear a strange scraping sound. For just a second it seems like these two things are somehow connected. But then I realize that the sound is coming from the shed door at the far side of the garden where Mr. Pete, that elderly Indian gentleman, is now standing with a hoe and a rake over his shoulder. I'm not sure if the sound I heard was the sound of the rake or the sound of the creaky shed door opening or the gruff sound Mr. Pete makes as he clears his throat, preparing to spit. Which he does now.

"Over there, Mr. Pete," Sister Sarah says, pointing to the end of the garden. "Loosen up the far row."

Sister Sarah looks at me and nods at the tangle of bushes

down there. "And pick some of those rose hips, Donna—just the tips. Good for congestion. Watch out for the thorns, though."

She walks toward the bushes and I follow, with Sister Mary Kate trailing behind us like a nervous shadow.

"Why don't you let those boys show you how to butcher the animal, the ones from up North?" Sister Sarah tells her. "Father Mullen says they're to earn their keep by hunting for us. Hasn't he told you this?"

Sister Mary Kate blushes and asks, "Which boys?" but before Sister Sarah can say, she answers the question herself. "The Aaluk brothers, probably. They're members of the Caribou Tribe, aren't they?"

Sister Sarah gives her a funny little smile. "Yes, I suspect they'd be the ones. They ought to know how to handle a slain moose easily enough."

Old man Pete, at the other end of the garden, snorts suddenly. He and Sister Sarah look at each other. It seems like both of them are trying not to laugh.

I concentrate on picking the rose hips. The thorns are so tiny, it's impossible to watch out for them the way Sister said to. And I'm too busy thinking about that moose, anyhow—imagining what it would be like to see a real one, high up on a mountain road. I think about how far a person could see, way up there in that wide-open white place, and right now I want, more than anything, to be up in the mountains watching the Aaluk boys butcher that slain moose, watching the whole world spread out before us down below.

I can feel Sister Sarah looking at me with those prickly old eyes of hers, and it seems like she's looking right down deep inside of me, somehow, looking at a place where nobody's ever looked before. I tug at a rose hip.

"And take Donna here," Sister says suddenly. "And some of the others. And maybe take a few of those young teachers, too. You'll need the help."

Sister Mary Kate looks at me, flustered, and says, "Yes, but . . ."

"It'll be good for them," Sister Sarah says.

Sister Mary Kate puts her arm around me and squares her shoulders as if she's made an important decision. "Surely not Donna," she says. "Donna doesn't want to see a bloody old moose."

I can't help it. I reach up quick and grab my Saint Christopher medal and run my finger across the numbers as hard as I can. "Yes I do," I say. "I really do want to see that moose."

I look at Sister Mary Kate. I think she's as surprised by what I've said as I am.

"Well, ah . . . all right then," she says.

I plunge my hands into the rose hips, watching Sister Mary Kate bustling off on her mission. My fingers are itching, but it's a good kind of itch, the kind of itch that makes you want to do something. Something important.

Burnt Offerings
SEPTEMBER 1961

LUKE

Mail comes at dinnertime. Father Flanagan brings it, swinging it into the cafeteria in that big brown leather bag of Father Mullen's. Whistling. We all watch that bag, which seems suddenly bigger than both Father Flanagan and Father Mullen put together. It's fat with the voices of our folks and the memories of home. Thick with the stories we tell ourselves, over and over, to make the bad things go away and make the good ones stay.

We don't hardly ever get mail, me and Bunna. Not like Chickie. Chickie's dad sends her lots of stuff from his store—hard candy and Sailor Boy crackers and raspberry jam. Sonny gets dried fish sometimes, which smells like smoke but tastes almost as good as our dried fish. Amiq gets weird stuff, like books and newspapers from this scientist who used to live in Barrow. The newspapers Amiq gets always have stories about Eskimos in them. We never knew, before this, that Eskimos could be in newspapers.

Junior's mail is the best, though. Junior gets tapes with peoples' voices on them, telling stories. Reel-to-reel tapes like the kind that have movies on them, only smaller. Tapes rolled up so tight with words, you could stretch them all the way from Junior's village to Sacred Heart and back. Tapes with his auntie talking about how his uncle Patrick's crew caught a whale and his cousin Daisy—the one who had a baby boy— jumped for the first time on the sealskin blanket. Junior's tapes have people singing songs and playing the drums, too. With Junior's tapes you can almost see them dancing Eskimo dances. His tapes tell about what the leaders there are doing, too, like how they stopped the government from trying to blow up atomic bombs by Point Hope. One of Junior's uncles wrote a long letter to the newspaper about it, and Junior is proud. We're proud, too.

We listen with the machine in the library and afterward Junior fills those tapes back up again with his own words— stories about Sacred Heart. *Our stories.* Junior tells how the dorms look and what kind of food the cafeteria has. He tells them things like how the river is frozen here and how we just learned to skate last week. We skated mostly on our butts, all right, which is exactly how Junior tells it.

Stories can make you laugh so hard it hurts sometimes and make you remember the good things so much it makes your throat get tight.

Today is going to be a good day and a good story for Junior to tell—the story about our first time hunting at Sacred Heart

School. And it starts right here in this shower room, where me and Bunna are shivering because even though we aren't dirty, they make us take showers all the darn time, which is dumb because everyone knows that when you wash every speck of dirt off your body, it makes you get cold easier, especially now, with winter coming—and when you get cold, you get sick. You can't be a good hunter if you're cold and sick all the time, and you can't catch animals when you smell like soap, either.

But the moose we're going after today already got caught—caught by a truck. And now it's lying dead on the side of the Sacred Heart road, and Father Mullen says I'm the hunter, so I gotta show them how to skin it. Truth is, I never even seen a moose before.

I step out of the shower the same time as Bunna, and the cold air hits us like ice water. We almost knock each other over grabbing at our towels. Bunna can't hardly stop shivering.

"*Alapaa!*"

He says it without thinking, then gets real scared, looking around quick like he expects something bad to happen. Like maybe Father Mullen's gonna step out from one of the stalls with his ruler and slap our butts. Tell us how we'll never get to Heaven because we aren't good Catholics.

All of a sudden I'm thinking about our little brother Isaac again, and my breathing gets trapped inside my chest.

"He's gone to a good Catholic home," Sister Sarah said. These are the only words she said that time, and they were not good words. Not the words that Mom wanted to hear, either. Mom cried when she found out about Isaac, and when Jack tried to hold her, she hit him, and the next thing we knew, Jack was gone.

I told Mom I'd find Isaac, but I don't know how.

"It's okay, Luke, it's okay," Sister Mary Kate said. "You have the faith of Abraham, remember that."

But it's not okay and I don't want Abraham's faith. I want my brother. Abraham's the one who tied up his own son and got ready to give him to God as a burnt offering, but then God gave him an old sheep to burn instead. Abraham's son was named Isaac, too, just like our brother. Only God never stopped them from taking *our* Isaac away the way he stopped Abraham from burning *his* Isaac. Which is why I got no use for God. I figure if he's gonna do stuff like that for one Isaac and not for another, then he isn't fair. And if he's going to do it to a little kid like our Isaac, then God is just plain mean, like Father Mullen, because Isaac been waiting his whole life to get big enough to learn how to hunt, and now he's gone, so he'll never learn anything. Not even how to skin a dumb old moose. Which me and Bunna are supposed to know how to do.

Bunna's thinking about it, too. Standing there with his teeth chattering, he says, "How we gonna skin a moose? We never even seen one before."

"Never mind," I say.

"Never mind" is what Mom always says when she doesn't want to think too hard about something.

Bunna looks at me. "But how we gonna figure it out?" he says. He says it like he knows I have the answer.

I don't, but I don't say this to Bunna. Bunna expects me to just take care of it somehow, like I'm supposed to take care of everything, which makes me think about Isaac, again, his face pressed against the back window of the car, disappearing into the trees that time, and about me and Bunna running away through those same trees and getting caught, and Father saying it's our job to go out there and hunt for them. Somehow I'm always supposed to take care of it, but how?

And all of a sudden, I'm mad. Mad enough to hit somebody. Hit Father Mullen, maybe. Hard.

Instead, I box at Bunna—Bunna, wrapped in his towel, his hair standing up every which way. Bunna ducks and laughs and tries to box back.

You can't get mad when you box. That's what Father Mullen says. When you box, you have to put all your feelings away, because if you let your feelings get in the way, you might make mistakes.

Father Mullen never makes mistakes.

Father is perfect when he boxes, like a dancer moving just right to the beat of the drum. Like the dancers I can see when Junior plays his tapes, dancers moving to the sound of the drums until the beat of the drum and the movement of their bodies turns into one thing, one perfect thing. I never figured out a word for that thing, but I see it in the way Father Mullen moves when he shows us how to box, boxing all by himself against a boxer nobody else can see. After a while that boxer gets so real, you could almost see the outline of his shadow, right there next to Father, throwing feints. Trying to fool him.

Father Mullen is never fooled.

The trick is to always be two moves ahead of your opponent.

That's what Father Mullen says, punching at his shadow.

That's why when Sister Mary Kate said I had to show them how to cut a moose, I never said I don't know how. Guess they think us boys up North are born with knives in our hands.

Guess it's okay to let them think that.

The trick is to always keep them guessing about what you know and what you don't know.

"But Luke," Bunna says again, "we don't know nothing about cleaning a moose."

The bathroom is still steamy from the showers, and the mirrors are all fogged up, so when you try to see yourself, it's like looking through smoke.

"Sure we do," I say, running my finger across the steamy mirror, watching Bunna's eyes pop out. "We watched Uncle Joe before, lotta times."

"Yeah, but that's caribou."

"So? Moose got four legs just like caribou. Cut them into pieces. Same way."

"Yeah, but how you get the skin off?"

"You pull, remember? The skin always pulls right off, like gloves."

"Yeah, but . . . you ever done it before?"

I sign my name on the mirror, taking time to make it neat.

"No, but you know how Mom always says it, right? We're Eskimo, and . . ."

". . . Eskimos know how to *survive*," Bunna chants.

I nod my head. "And that's exactly what we're gonna do."

L—u—k—e, I write. I make the tail of the "e" long and straight and draw a harpoon on the end, a hunter's harpoon. *We're gonna survive.*

Father Flanagan drives us out to find the dead moose. He drives the old Sacred Heart bus—military trash, Amiq calls it, because it was the bus the base was going to throw away but gave to us instead.

The birch trees shiver their skinny black branches against the sky, a straggling of yellow leaves clinging to them. Chickie and Donna sit in front of me, Donna by the window, her face pressed against the glass. I tap my foot on the floor, part nervous and part excited. Bunna looks at my foot, and when he sees the way I'm tapping, he starts acting nervous, too.

I quit tapping and shove my foot under the seat.

That's when I feel it—something under the seat, something soft and lumpy like a dead body. I bend down to see what it is, and Bunna bends down, too. Bunna sees it before I do: Father Mullen's mail bag. It looks smaller under there, like a little brown animal. Before I can stop him, Bunna slides it out and pulls it open. When we see what's in there, there's no stopping either one of us. Right on top is a letter that has my name on it: Luke Aaluk, handwritten in big square letters. And it's already been opened, too. Somebody with a razor-sharp knife has slit that letter all the way open, right along the top edge, side to side.

Suddenly the bus lurches, and everyone is standing up, trying to see out the window. Nobody sees me slide that letter into my pocket, easy as sliding a knife into its sheath. Nobody sees me kick that mail bag back under the seat. Everybody's too busy looking at something else.

"Up there. Right there!" somebody cries.

It's the moose, lying alongside the road, looking more like a brown gunnysack full of meat than something that used to run around. It's not as big as I thought, just long, spindly legs and a ribbed body.

"Why, it's just a baby!" one of the teachers cries.

"Man, they sure smashed it up," Bunna says.

But you can see it's mostly just the head that's smashed. The meat part looks okay. I take a deep breath as Father pulls off the road and wonder how I'm going to do this thing I never done before.

When we step down off the bus, the sun is shining cold, and the air smells cold, too, with little flecks of snow in it. The last of the leaves on the trees are yellow and browning, floating down from the branches like fur shedding, which is what trees do in the winter, I guess.

I'm glad to feel that wind, all right. We're higher up in the valley than the school, way up by the mountains. Up here you can feel the wind and see farther, too. You can even hear the sound of ravens, cawing way off in the distance, which makes me think of home. *Tulugaq*, that's what we call ravens.

Bunna and I stand together on the side of the road, looking down at the moose. Everybody is watching. Waiting. I shift from one foot to another, staring down at the dusty moose, wishing it had instructions stamped on its skin.

"All right, Luke, you're in charge," Father says.

I look up, eyeing a little patch of tundra on the other side of the road.

"First we better drag it over there, where we can work on it," I say, nodding at the spot of high tundra, just like Uncle Joe would. Cleaner than the dirt road.

Father takes one of the front legs and I take the other. Sister Mary Kate steps forward with a determined little smile and grabs a back leg, looking over at the volunteer teachers, who stand off to the side of the road with pale faces. Some of them look like they might get sick.

"Come on, girls," Sister calls. "Let's not shun Providence."

I'm not exactly sure what she means by that, but before any of the teachers can worry about shunning Providence, Donna steps up and grabs a leg, which really surprises me. Donna doesn't seem like the kind of girl who would want to get her hands dirty with a dead moose.

Together we pull that moose up onto the tundra. Then everyone stands back, waiting. I swallow a little lump of fear, running my finger along the blade of the knife Father gave me. Then I lean down and slit that moose open right up the belly, end to end, easy as unzipping a jacket. I breathe deep and smile.

The teachers all step backward with one movement. But the kids all step closer.

"My," says one of the teachers in a whispery voice.

Bunna moves in right next to me, squatting down with a grin.

See? I tell him with my eyes. Then I reach up inside the belly like I seen Uncle Joe do with caribou. But you have to reach a lot farther in to get inside a moose than you do with a caribou, even a baby moose. I'm in up to my shoulder before my hand finds the top edge of the guts. I pull hard, and the insides come sliding out just like water. One of the teachers behind me gasps.

"All right then, here's the heart," Father says, stepping forward and nodding down at my hand. I look at my hand and realize that I'm clutching that baby moose heart like it might save my life.

"Where's that sack, Sister?" Father calls.

Sister grabs one of the burlap sacks they brought, and Bunna reaches into the mess of guts and pulls out the *taqtuk* like he's done it a hundred times. Amiq winks at him.

"Here's the *taqtuk*," Bunna says. *Taqtuk* is Bunna's favorite. "What do Catholics call *taqtuk*, Luke?" Bunna whispers.

I don't know what Catholics call *taqtuk*, so I pretend I'm too busy to talk.

"*Taqtuk* is kidneys," Amiq says, tipping his head at Sister with a smile.

I know I'm supposed to take the skin off next, and I'm pulling with one hand and punching with the other, trying to separate the skin from the meat like I seen Joe do before with caribou, seen Mom do with fox, but the skin won't separate. It's stuck hard, like it's frozen onto the meat.

"You can't pull the skin off like it's a parka," Sonny says, laughing sharply, like the sound a *tulugaq* makes. He even looks like a raven. Bunna glares at him.

"I seen them pull the skins off caribous," Bunna mutters. "Lots of times."

"That look like a caribou to you?" Sonny says.

Amiq moves over and squats down next to us.

"Naw," he says, watching Sonny with a sharp eye. "That ain't no caribou. Stinks like a wet dog."

Sonny glares at Amiq like he's just insulted his mother. This makes me laugh, which makes Sonny glare even harder.

"Of course it's different with moose," I say smoothly. "With moose you got to cut it up into pieces first, then take the skin off."

Sonny gets a funny look on his face like he thinks maybe I'm bluffing but isn't quite sure. That's when I realize that Sonny don't know any more about cleaning a moose than we do. Heck, Sonny probably don't even know we don't got moose in our village. How could he? He's never been that far north, I bet.

Even when it's cut up into pieces, taking the skin off a moose isn't easy. You have to use a knife all the way through, separating the skin from the meat very carefully. By the time I reach the last piece, I got it down cold, and everybody is looking at me like I'm the expert. Heck, maybe I am. I'm the new expert moose skinner of Sacred Heart School.

In the cafeteria that night, we eat fried moose meat with gravy, proud of ourselves. It's not caribou, all right, but it tastes okay. Good, almost. Then Father Mullen comes striding through the cafeteria, whistling. Swinging that mail bag of his. He likes to act like he's just walking through the room for fun, but the whole room explodes with the sound of kids calling out, "Who's got a letter?" "Whose package?" That letter I pulled out of the mail bag without asking is getting very heavy, and I haven't even been able to read it yet.

"Hey, look what I got," Amiq hollers.

It's a newspaper clipping. Amiq unfolds it and lays it out on the table for everyone to see. There's a picture of a bunch of Iñupiaq guys in a line. It's not our village, but me and Bunna recognize some of them. The guy at the front of the line is signing an official-looking paper. Off to the side, closer, is a guy with a big smile holding a duck. I'd recognize that smile anywhere.

"Hey! That's my uncle Joe!" I shout.

Bunna leans over, and we read the headline together: "Eskimos in Game Law Revolt," it says.

"What's that mean?" Bunna asks.

Amiq laughs. "It means your uncle is a good man, Bunna."

Kids are crowding around to read the story about the Eskimo revolt, but not me. I've gone back to thinking about *my* letter, the one sitting in my pocket with my name on it, unread. The one I'm afraid to take out of my pocket. But right now that letter is the only story I'm interested in reading.

We have to wait a long time to read it, though, me and Bunna. We wait until after dinner, when we're all alone in our room, after all them other guys arc in the showers.

When we realize it's a letter from our little brother Isaac, we hardly dare breathe for fear somebody's gonna catch us before we get a chance to finish it.

DEAR BROTHER,

MY NEW HOUSE HAS A TREE. I KNOW HOW TO CLIMB MY TREE. DAD IS GOING TO BUILD A TREE HOUSE. IT IS HOT HERE AND WE GO SWIMMING.

SINCERELY,
ISAAC

PS HOW COME YOU NEVER ANSWER MY LETTERS?

Those last words make me clench my fists up tight.

The letter has no return address, and I never got no other letters, so how could I answer them? But there's a postmark on it. I study it close, trying to figure out what it means. It's a circle with a date in the center—AUG 15, 1961—and the word TEX at the bottom. That means Texas, I'm sure. There's a city name on the top, but I can't read it because it's smudged. Part of it says DA.

When I slip that letter back into its envelope, the sight of that knife-cut edge along the top makes me boxing mad.

"Your opponent will always have a weak spot," Father Mullen says. "Don't ever forget that."

When I think about Isaac swimming in some hot place, I feel cold and my chest gets tight, because swimming is like a weak spot for us. Us Eskimos are not swimmers. If we fall into the ocean back home, we don't swim. We get pulled out quick before the cold kills us.

At least Isaac is okay, though. You could tell he's okay by the way he makes his letters, real neat, forming the words as smooth as leaves falling.

How'd Isaac learn how to climb a tree, anyhow?

"What are we going to do with the letter?" Bunna whispers.

For some reason, I think of Abraham getting ready to burn his son Isaac.

"We gotta burn it," I say, imagining what Father Mullen would do if he found out we took it.

"How come?"

"Never mind," I whisper.

Father Mullen is teaching us boys to be boxers all right, and that's okay by us, too. We will always stay two moves ahead of our opponent, and we will always look for his weak spot. And we will not throw any punches until we have a clear shot, no matter how long it takes. Father didn't have to teach us that one; we already knew because we're hunters.

"But how we gonna burn that letter when we don't even got matches?" Bunna says.

Never mind. We'll find a way. We will always find a way.

Military Trash
MARCH 1962

CHICKIE

It's snowing outside, making everything in the whole world seem bright and quiet, and I have a new diary. Swede sent it to me, and I'm trying to write in it, trying to record things, which is just about impossible, bouncing down this frozen road in our beat-up old bus. We are returning from a trip to Fairbanks, where our basketball team beat the team at the Catholic school there. We won because Sonny is tough and Amiq is fast and Michael O'Shay, that new boy, is just plain tall.

"Dear Diary," I write, but the "a" and "i" get turned around and it says, "Dear Dairy." Which makes me mad because I've written it in ink, and there is no turning back. I'm writing to a dairy instead of a diary. *Dumb!*

I look out at the falling snow, glittering in the late after-noon, and I feel warm and protected somehow. It's getting close to dinner, and the boys are talking about food, and even though the snow outside muffles us, they are managing to make more noise than a herd of elephants, which is typical of boys.

"Man, I sure wish Sister knew how to make caribou soup like Mom," Bunna says.

"Or dry fish like my grandpa," Leo Pete says. Leo Pete lives right by the school, and his grandpa catches salmon in the river. Leo's grandpa is the one Luke and Bunna are afraid of, even though they don't ever say it.

Amiq snorts.

"Why don't you pups worry 'bout something more likely, like maybe Sister Sarah's gonna turn into an astronaut?"

Luke and Sonny start to laugh at this one until they suddenly realize they are both laughing at the same thing, which makes them start to frown instead. I swear, those two. Always bristling like dogs over the same bone. And Amiq's holding the bone. As usual.

"Who you calling a *pup*?" Leo asks, narrowing his eyes.

Amiq nudges Junior, sitting in the seat right next to him, his nose stuck in a book. As usual.

"Hey, Junior, you hear some yapping?"

Junior looks up, pushing his glasses up on his nose all dreamyeyed.

"Mapping?" he says, and everybody laughs, even Sonny and Luke together.

That's the thing about Junior. He's kind of on everybody's team. I mean he's so spacey, it's like he's in a totally different universe. He never takes one side or the other. Like a referee without a whistle, he just kind of drifts around on the edge of the game.

"I am traveling in an old bus with a bunch of wild boys who are making a bunch of noise about nothing," I write.

All of a sudden there's a sound like a gun going off, and Sister Mary Kate jumps up like she's been shot. The bus sputters to a stop, and there's total silence. Father Flanagan leans out from the driver's seat.

"Not to worry, boys and girls, not to worry," Father calls out. "Just a spot of engine trouble, nothing to fret over."

He looks out over the top of his glasses at Sister Mary Kate, who, of course, blushes. Then he jumps down out of the bus, and the boys all crane their necks, trying to see what he's doing. I'm guessing pretty much every boy on this bus knows more about engines than Father.

"Our bus broke down, and Father is going to fix it," I write.

"Man," Bunna mutters. "Why can't we have a real bus, like the kind they have at *real* schools?"

"Now, Bunna," Sister Mary Kate says, "we must not covet what others have. We must be grateful for the Providence the Lord has provided."

"Oh, Lord," Amiq says, folding his hands and looking up toward the roof of the bus with what he thinks is a pious look. "Thank you for providing us with military trash. We are not worthy."

Sister acts like she doesn't hear him, but you can tell she

does by the way she looks out the window and frowns. Amiq is lucky Father Mullen's not here.

"Stay put, girls and boys, stay put," Sister says, wringing her hands and glancing nervously out the window of the bus. "I need to assist Father."

Evelyn makes a funny noise, and Rose covers her mouth with her hand. I figure pretty much any Indian girl in the world knows more about engines than Sister.

Of course as soon as Sister steps off the bus, the boys start going crazy as loons. Sam Pete grabs my diary with his grubby little paws, and just as I'm getting ready to pound him to pieces, he tosses it back to his brother, Leo, but Leo misses it and it hits Junior, hits him right square on the head. Junior looks up, annoyed and owlish, but before he can figure out what's happened, Leo slides into Junior's seat like it's home plate and grabs the diary. Then he and Sam start playing catch with it, lobbing it back and forth the length of the bus, and the harder I holler, the faster they throw.

All of a sudden here's Bunna, popping up in the middle of it all like an Eskimo jack-in-the-box, grabbing my diary midair.

"You lose something, Snowbird?" he says, tucking my diary into his stinky old armpit and throwing himself down onto his seat where he sits, slowly opening it up and sticking his nose right inside the front page, right into the part where it says, "Property of Chickie Snow. DO NOT OPEN."

He lifts the page and gives me an evil grin.

"BUN-NA!"

"Hey, I saved your old book, didn't I? Least you could do is let me read it."

I fly at him like a banshee, hollering my head off. "Bunna, you dirty animal, I'm gonna choke you."

He's laughing so hard he almost *is* choking, ducking his head like he's avoiding a blow and holding his hand in front of his fat face.

"I jokes," he says, handing me the diary. "What do I want your silly old book for, anyway?"

I grab my diary, flying backward and bashing into Junior with a force strong enough to knock his big black-rimmed glasses clear off his face. Junior looks up just in time to watch his second eyes go sailing across to the other side the bus, where they dash into the window next to that new white kid, Michael O'Shay. O'Shay leans down a long arm and starts groping around on the floor for them.

"Sh . . . sh . . . SHAVING CREAM!" Junior cries.

Rose and Evelyn start giggling.

"That's right, Junior, let it all out," Amiq coos.

Rose and Evelyn are laughing so hard, they're almost crying.

Junior glares at me like it's all my fault. "What are you try-ing to do, k . . . kill me?"

Right then Michael O'Shay emerges victorious, handing me the glasses.

"Look, Junior, they're okay," I offer.

Junior grabs them defensively, adjusting the nose piece as he shoves them back on his face.

"Jeez, Snowbird, create a ruckus, will you?" Bunna says.

I spin around, ready to deck him, and he raises his hand again.

"Hey! Don't ruffle your . . ."

He stops midsentence. We all stop because we all realize, suddenly, that Sister Mary Kate is standing at the front door of the bus, glaring at us. Well, maybe you wouldn't really call it a glare. Sister doesn't know how to glare. But that's what she intends, I'm sure.

"Ladies! Gentlemen! Please!"

I slink back to my seat.

Sister sets her hands on her hips like she wants us to believe she means business, when of course we all know Sister doesn't have the slightest idea how to mean business. Especially not with a bunch of kids nearly swinging from the rafters of a rickety old piece of a military-trash bus.

"Father has suggested that you children need my guidance more than he does right now," she says, narrowing her eyes at me and Bunna. "And I do believe he's right."

She stands there, arms crossed, looking at us with what she probably figures is a stern expression, and all of us make a real effort to settle down, even though we all know Sister couldn't hurt a flea.

"Children, let's recite the Twenty-third Psalm," Sister says, launching into it with fervor.

"'The Lord is my shepherd," she announces, looking at us girls, waiting for us to catch up with our good voices, which we do, of course, because we know full well that the boys couldn't manage the words to the Twenty-third Psalm to save their sorry souls.

"... and I shall not want," we all chime in.

Right then the door to the bus opens with a breath of cool air, and Father steps inside, brushing snow from his sleeves.

"Behold the shepherd," Amiq announces, like he's a narrator in a Christmas play or something.

Sister drops the psalm like a hot potato, crying, "Father! You fixed it!"

"God willing, Sister. God willing."

The boys give each other looks that say, *God's will wouldn't touch a project like this with a ten-foot pole.* Then there's total silence as Father takes to the driver's seat. When he turns the key, we all strain right along with that engine.

"Come on girl, you can do it," Bunna says. Like he was talking to a dog or something. "Come on."

Father keeps right on cranking away, but that engine doesn't make a sound, not even a mutter.

That's when I remember just how long a walk it is back to the school. "Come on," I whisper. "*Come on.*"

Father lets up on the brakes, and the bus starts to roll down the hill, easy at first, then bouncing a little on the rocky road. The engine gives a little sputter like a dog sneezing, and then it starts to kick in. As the bus gathers speed, Sister orders us all to pray, clutching the side of her chair with her eyes clenched shut like she's afraid to even look.

"Yea though I walk through the valley of the shadow of death, I shall fear no evil . . ."

She's praying so fast that the psalm takes off like a snow-ball down a hill, and I get so caught up in the momentum that before she comes to the end, I accidentally say, "Amen" ahead of everybody else.

Bunna laughs, looking right at me with that evil little grin of his.

I open up my diary and write "BUNNA A IS A DUMB ANIMAL." Then, just for good measure, I underlined every word twice, pressing especially hard: "BUNNA A IS A DUMB ANIMAL." That's when I realize I have accidentally added an extra A. But that's okay; Bunna's last name is Aaluk, so "Bunna A" makes sense.

I snap the book shut, happy in the knowledge that I have recorded a thing for all posterity, as Sister would say last name and all.

Meanwhile, the bus limps along in the snow-bright dark-ness, headed down the mountain, straight for Sacred Heart.

The Day the Soldiers Came
APRIL 5, 1962, 8:00 A.M.

LUKE

Bunna is standing by the window in the hallway of the dorm, his nose pressed up against the glass. That white kid, O'Shay, is leaning over top of him, and both of them are staring out the window without hardly moving. Like the yard's full of moose or something. Bunna turns around when he hears me.

"Soldiers," he hisses.

I go look out, and sure enough, it's soldiers: jeeps, uniforms, and all.

"What the heck," I say.

"Maybe the Russians have invaded," O'Shay says, grinning.

Bunna moves away from the window fast.

"Aw, c'mon," O'Shay says. "You don't really believe that stuff, do you?"

Bunna frowns like he thinks O'Shay is making fun of him.

I tell O'Shay, "Back home, when the sky gets real red over

the ocean, our mom always says it could be Russia burning."

Bunna nods.

"No way," O'Shay says.

"Way," Bunna says.

Guess O'Shay don't know what it's like living on the coast across from Russia. He's from Fairbanks, which is what they call the Interior, and it's about a thousand miles from the ocean. Besides, he's white.

"We got Russian subs out there in our ocean all the time," I tell him. "Just under the surface, like killer whales."

"Killer whales," O'Shay says. "That's a good one."

"You aren't supposed to joke about killer whales," Bunna says.

"I wasn't joking about killer whales," O'Shay says.

"Yeah, 'cause the way it is with killer whales, they never forget the people who tease them," I say. "There's a guy making fun of them whales one year, and two years later, whales surround his boat and he's dead." It's true, too.

We look out the window. The soldiers are marching right up into the school.

"Least they're on our side," Bunna says.

I breathe deep. No kidding. Least they're on our side. But what the heck are they protecting us from? It's a question I don't really want to think about, but I do anyhow. I think about it all through breakfast, and it follows me down the hall and into class, where it lurks just under the surface, like a killer whale. How can Father Flanagan stand there spouting Latin like nothing's happening?

"*O filii mei boni bellifera,*" Father says loudly. "What does it mean? Anyone?"

Chickie giggles and Evelyn snorts because it sounds like he's saying, "O feely me boney belly" with some kind of accent. Junior shoves his glasses onto his nose and clears his throat.

"Junior?"

"Oh my great warring son," Junior says fast, his voice cracking.

"Good. Very good."

Father writes those words on the blackboard in neat writing. Then he looks up over our heads toward the door. Seeing the expression on his face, we all turn around and stare. Father Mullen stands just outside the door, waiting.

"I want you to turn to chapter six, class, and get started," Father Flanagan tells us. "I'll be right with you."

Everybody makes a show of turning pages, but all of us are really watching Father Mullen and Father Flanagan talking together just outside the door. We can't see no good reason for Mullen to interrupt the class like that, and we know that wherever Mullen goes, trouble follows sure as snow.

Father returns to the class, rubbing his hands like he's trying to warm them.

"All right, then," he says. "All right. Slight change of plans, boys and girls. Slight change. I need a few of you for testing."

"You didn't tell us there was going to be a test, Father," O'Shay says nervously.

O'Shay's dad is real strict about his grades. Not like the rest of us. The rest of us passed our parents' grade levels about five years ago, so our parents think we're geniuses no matter what kinds of grades we get. But O'Shay's dad is a lawyer, and O'Shay's grades are never good enough.

"Not that kind of test, Michael," Father says. "This test is more like an eye test."

Evelyn looks at Junior's glasses, suspicious. "Whatsa matter with our eyes?"

"Nothing. Nothing at all," Father says. "I didn't say it *was* an eye test, I said it's *like* an eye test. And it's only a few of you that will need to be tested. Not to worry."

But I get a funny feeling watching the way Father goes through his grade book, running his finger over the page like he's looking for something hidden.

"Luke Aaluk," he says, and I stand up, not knowing what else to do.

"Donna Anaivik," he continues without looking up.

Donna stands up, eyeing her feet.

" . . . Billy Stone, Jr., . . . Fred Qavik."

Father looks up and then back down at his grade book. "Let's see. Have I forgotten anyone?"

Amiq stands up while Father is still running his finger over our names, searching.

"Oh . . . yes . . . Amiq," he says finally, looking straight at Amiq, who's standing directly in front of him, as cool and calm as only Amiq can be. "Amiq Amundson."

"Eskimos front and center, eh, Father?" Amiq says.

"It would appear so, Amiq. It would indeed appear so."

But it isn't all Eskimos. Out in the hallway there's other kids, even Indians from the villages up north by ours, even the kids from the lower levels, all of us standing around, eyes big. Bunna moves up next to me.

"All right, ladies and gentlemen, form a line," Sister Sarah orders.

We march down the hall behind the white flag of Sister's habit like a blind army. Where we're going and what we're fighting is a mystery none of us wants to think about. Sister stops at a little room next to the office, a room that's mostly used for storage because it's too small for a classroom and doesn't have a window.

"All right people, I want you to remain in line here. You'll be called in one at a time for testing," Sister Sarah says.

And sure enough, right after she disappears into the room, one of those soldiers ducks his head out and looks directly at me.

"Luke Aaluk?"

"Yes, sir."

"Looks like you're the leader."

And I'm thinking, *Why the heck did I have to be first? I'm not even a Catholic.* Should've been somebody else, somebody daring like Amiq. I don't believe in being daring. Daring people are just dumb people who never live long. Not in the Arctic.

But Amiq's not first in line. I am. Amiq's at the dead end of the line, in fact, and he's scowling. I'm the leader, with Bunna right behind me, which is not right, that's for sure. But I lift my shoulders up and march right into that room, my mouth dry as sand.

Inside is two soldiers who say they're doctors. They have a table full of equipment.

Sister Sarah eases the door shut, leaving me alone with the military. I stand there in the middle of that room, an army of one, trying to look tough.

"Sit down, son," one of the soldiers says. "This isn't going to hurt one bit."

It don't feel right when he calls me "son," but I sit down anyway. He sits down, too, across the table from me.

"My name is Dr. Smith, Luke, and I need you to hold real still while Dr. Bergstrom here hooks you up to his machine," he says.

Suddenly I'm more curious than scared. "Why are you hooking me up to a machine?"

"So we can learn a few things about your body," he says.

The way he talks about my body is like it's not connected to me, not real. And the way he's taping these little wires onto me makes me feel like Frankenstein, that guy in a movie they showed one time.

Dr. Bergstrom connects wires to all my fingertips, the sides of my forehead, the back of my neck, my heart, even my ankles.

"Learn what kinds of things?"

The two doctors are putting on heavy aprons and gloves, and one is opening up a big silver-colored box. He takes out a container and pours something into a paper cup.

"The military wants to know what it is about your body that allows you to adapt so well to extreme cold. You kids are going to show us how to condition our soldiers to fight better in the extreme cold of the Arctic."

He hands me the cup. The liquid inside is greenish yellow and fluorescent-looking. I'm wondering how this stuff could teach anybody to fight. And why do they have to fight in the Arctic, anyhow? Did the Russians land already? I think about Mom and get scared.

"Here. Drink this juice."

I look at it doubtfully. "What is it?"

"It's iodine-131, Luke. Do you know what that is?"

I shake my head. Iodine-131 doesn't look like anything I would ever want to drink.

"Iodine-131 is what we call a radioactive tracer, Luke. When it runs through your body, we'll be following the radiation levels with our machines here, and it will tell us a lot about your body and how it works."

I look at the "juice." Iodine-131 is no juice name I ever heard of.

"Go ahead, Luke, drink it. It won't hurt. They tell me it tastes pretty good, in fact."

They're both looking at me like they plan to stand there, looking forever if they have to, which makes me real uncomfortable, so I take the cup and swallow it down.

He's right. It don't taste too bad.

"Taste okay?"

I nod my head.

"Want another?"

I say no so fast it makes them chuckle, the one guy taking the cup and putting it back inside the metal container, the other removing his gloves and watching the machine. They don't take those aprons off.

"What kind of aprons are those?" I ask, because they look heavy, different from any apron I ever saw.

"Lead," one of them says. "Keeps the radiation out."

I swallow, wondering how come they want to keep the radiation out of them but not me. The other doctor just looks back at me, staring me right in the eye and smiling slow and easy.

"See, everyone has a touch of radiation in their bodies, Luke. That's why we have to wear these aprons—to keep our natural radiation from interfering with the results of this test. We want to measure *your* radiation level, not ours."

I look at them with those heavy aprons, wondering what a radiation level is.

"You're like a soldier, now, son," he says, slugging me soft on the shoulder. "You're a soldier in the army's Cold War."

I'm still wondering about being a soldier when they open the door and let me out. Bunna is standing there next in line, his eyes big as baseballs, his body tense. I grin.

"It's okay," I tell him. "They're on our side. And it don't hurt."

I turn around so all the others can see, too. "See? No bandages!"

Bunna looks me up and down and grins.

I go on down the line, nodding at the other guys until I get to Amiq at the end of the line. Amiq grabs me by the shoulders. Hard.

"What's in there?" he whispers real sharp.

"It's nothing," I tell him. "Just two doctors and some machines. They put a bunch of wires on you and make you drink this juice and then they sit there watching their machines. It don't hurt."

"What kind of *juice*," Amiq says, spitting out the word *juice* like it's burned his tongue. "What kind?"

"I don't know. Iodine something. Iodine-131. It's a weird green color."

"*Jesus,*" Amiq says, and the way he says it makes my skin crawl, makes me turn and look at Bunna, suddenly scared.

But Bunna's already on his way into the room, and I can feel that green juice starting to boil inside me like battery acid. I turn back to ask Amiq about it, but Amiq's gone now, too. Just like that.

Back in class, Father Flanagan looks us over carefully in a way that makes me feel weird. Father frowns when he sees Amiq's empty seat.

"His stomach was bothering him, Father. I think maybe he's gone to the infirmary," I say. I don't even know what made me say it; it just came out, like a hiccup. Lying.

Junior looks at me, nervous.

"They made us drink a green substance, Father," Junior says. "Maybe it didn't agree with him."

"They did?" Chickie asks, looking at Bunna.

"Tasted sweet, and kinda oily," Bunna says, wrinkling his nose.

Father Flanagan gets a funny look on his face like he doesn't want to hear any more. Then he opens his Latin book and strides over to the blackboard.

"All right then," he says.

"Father?" Junior says.

There's a new sound in Junior's voice, a concern that even Father hears. He turns around, head cocked, looking at Junior. Waiting.

"Did they ask our parents about those tests, Father? Did our parents give permission?"

Father looks startled. "Why yes, Junior, I'm sure they did." But his voice don't sound sure. Not at all.

Bunna and I look at each other. We know our mom, and we don't figure she'd say it's okay to make us drink some kind of oily green stuff that looks like it could just about glow in the dark. But Mom would trust soldiers, just like she trusted the Church with Isaac. She always would.

"But, of course, you know, the school acts *in loco parentis* while you kids are here," Father says.

In loco parentis. I know those words somehow. I feel them. It is not a good feeling.

"What's that mean?" Bunna asks.

"It's Latin," Father says. "Let's figure it out."

"In place of parents," Junior says quietly.

"The school is here for us in place of our parents," O'Shay adds.

"Right," says Father. "Quite right."

For some reason, thinking about Mom makes me think about Uncle Joe and hunting, which makes me remember about the killer whales. Uncle Joe says killer whales understand Iñupiaq, and if you're a good person and you ask, they'll help.

Even though we're about a thousand miles away from the sea, I can feel them out there, just under the surface of things. Waiting.

The Meanest Heathens

APRIL 5, 1962, 8:00 A.M.

SONNY AND AMIQ

The soldiers had showed up at the cafeteria that day, right in the middle of breakfast, right before they started testing kids. They had stood with their backs against the wall, standing right next to Father Mullen, their faces blank as bullets. They reminded Sonny of hunters, the way they followed kids with their eyes, hardly moving a muscle.

Creepy.

Sonny cleared his tray, following right behind O'Shay, one eye on those soldiers. He wished that he and O'Shay could just disappear, but they were the wrong kind of kids for that. O'Shay was just too danged tall and too white. And Sonny— well, Sonny had that thing the oldest boy in a family without a dad always has, the thing that makes you act a certain way even when you don't really want to. The thing that makes older people treat you like an adult no matter how old you are.

"O'Shay!" Father Mullen said suddenly, and O'Shay stopped short, right in front of Mullen.

Sonny stopped, too. He had no choice. O'Shay and Father were blocking the way.

Father had a big, friendly smile on his face that looked about as natural as frosting on a fish. And the way he was rubbing his hands together made even O'Shay fidget. The soldier standing next to Father wore a fancy hat, and he had a row of stars on his arm that you couldn't help but notice because of the way he held his shoulder: right in your face.

"Mr. O'Shay, I'd like you to help me give the general here a tour of the school," Mullen said.

O'Shay gave Sonny a sideways look and swallowed. "Ah, maybe Sonny . . ."

Father nodded and looked at Sonny. "You come, too, Mr. George," Father said.

And that's how they ended up on a tour, Sonny and O'Shay and Father Mullen, marching that starred general through the halls of Sacred Heart School like a mismatched battalion from an unnamed war. Father was talking about the design of the school, striding past the row of photographs that showed the ranks of Sacred Heart graduates. The general gazed at the photos, then turned to scrutinize O'Shay.

"Your father is an attorney in Fairbanks, I hear," the general said.

O'Shay nodded. "Yes, sir."

"A prominent Catholic family," Father added.

"And you"—the general turned and looked down his shoulder, aiming his gaze at Sonny—"where are you from, young man?"

"Tannana, Sir."

"Indian," Father Mullen offered.

The general's face brightened a bit. "Bought my wife a pair of those Indian slippers," the general said, looking at Sonny like he expected gratitude. "Been complaining about cold feet ever since we got here. Warm as all get out, those slippers of yours."

Sonny shifted from one foot to the other.

They were outside now, standing next to the north wall of the school, and Father had stopped by the place where the new addition was going to be.

"This is the site of the new dorm wing. In fact, some of these boys here will help us build It," Father said, looking directly at Sonny.

Sonny'd be helping, all right. He never left summers—what else was there to do? The general was staring at him in a way that made him feel itchy.

"Good to see these Native boys learn useful trades," the general said.

Sonny forced a smile. A useful kind of smile. And he made himself look directly at the general, too, the way white people always did.

"Personable young fellow," the general said.

O'Shay, standing behind Mullen and the general, nodded knowingly at Sonny and grinned. *Personable.* He mouthed the word at Sonny.

What the heck does personable *mean?* Sonny wondered. *That the general thinks I could maybe be a person?*

The exterior of the school rose up alongside them, gray as ash, and Sonny thought about his mother's beadwork, the bright blue and red flowers she always put on the toes of her slippers. What would his mom think if she could see him standing here next to Father Mullen with a big, important general and the son of a prominent Fairbanks lawyer? She'd be pretty darn proud, Sonny decided.

"Would you like to see the chapel, sir?" he asked.

Outside the room where the soldiers were still testing kids, Amiq stood at the end of the line, waiting. He had just watched the way Luke marched into that room, like he was facing a firing squad, and now Amiq stood there feeling very . . . uneasy.

They were making them take some kind of military test, but it was only the kids who lived north of the Arctic Circle who had to take it. Amiq had figured this out by looking at the other kids standing there in line with them. They were Iñupiaq, mostly, with a few Indians—but only the ones who lived in the northernmost villages. There were no white kids.

Amiq had grown up around military scientists, and he knew all about military *testing*. Now they wanted to test him like he was some kind of lab animal. Amiq knew all about lab animals, too. This was not good. Not at all good.

Luke emerged from the testing room looking a little shaken and trying to cover it up by showing his brother Bunna how it hadn't even hurt.

"See? No bandage!" he told Bunna.

There are worse things than bandages, Amiq thought. The

whole thing made him feel angry and voiceless. He wanted to shout some sense into them all. Instead he just grabbed Luke by the shoulders as he walked by and made him tell exactly what they'd done to him. That's how he found out about the iodine-131. They were making kids drink it. Amiq didn't know exactly what iodine-131 was, but there was no way in Hell he was going to drink it.

Sonny wasn't quite sure what to think about this whole testing thing. The way Father Flanagan had explained it in class seemed odd. And the way he'd said the word *test* gave Sonny the willies. But it was only the kids from way up north who had to get tested. Not him, and not the Pete boys. Not Rose and Evelyn, either. Part of him was real glad that it wasn't his people. The other part was . . . well, it was complicated.

He tried to sort it out as he headed back to his room. Father Mullen had told Sonny and O'Shay that they could skip class while the other kids got tested because they'd been such good guides. The way he said it made Sonny squirm. But it was okay to have a few moments of freedom, even if it was almost lunchtime. Maybe they could eat lunch with the general, Father had said, smiling that cold smile of his. O'Shay had warmed to this idea because O'Shay liked being a big shot. O'Shay, in fact, was already on his way down to the cafeteria. But Sonny had a bad feeling in the pit of his stomach, and when he thought of eating lunch with the general, that feeling got heavy as a rock. Maybe he'd skip lunch today. Then he thought of his mom and how proud she'd be to see him eating lunch with a real live general, and he decided that he'd just go back to his room for a few minutes first.

He saw Amiq as soon he turned the corner. Amiq was standing by the entrance to the dorm wing. He was acting funny, tucked up inside the dorm hallway, his back pressed up against the wall, not moving. Not hardly breathing, even. Not acting at all the way that little loudmouth usually acted. Down the hall, the general was advancing like a tank. He had a stack of papers in his hands, and his head was bent so far into those papers, he didn't even see Amiq. Amiq looked like he wanted to disappear, but there was no place to hide, and the general was closing in fast—but he was studying those papers so hard, it looked like he might walk right on by Amiq without even seeing him. And you could tell for sure that's exactly what Amiq was counting on.

All of a sudden, Sonny realized that he was counting on the same thing, holding his breath right along with Amiq. As if he, too, were standing there right next to Amiq, hiding from the general. The general walked by Amiq and kept right on walking, walking without even looking up. Like he couldn't even see Amiq standing there, trying to act like a wall. Then, without any warning, the general stopped short and looked up. Like a hunter who's heard the sudden crack of a branch. Something about the idea of the general as a hunter was really creepy and without thinking about it, Sonny started to walk fast. Toward Amiq. He could hear the general's voice now.

"Aren't you one of the Eskimos?" the general was saying. "Aren't you supposed to be there with the rest of them?"

Sonny couldn't ever remember seeing Amiq get speechless, and if it weren't for the wolfish look on the general's face, he would have enjoyed it. As it was, Amiq's silence felt suffocating.

Without knowing he was going to do it, Sonny smiled right at the general and said in a loud, firm voice, "It's okay. He's my brother, sir."

The general turned, surprised, but when he saw who it was—*his Indian guide*—he smiled real big. Sonny smiled right back at him with what Sister Mary Kate always called his million-dollar smile.

Amiq stood there by the wall, practically gasping. Like a fish out of water.

"This one's no Eskimo, sir. He's my brother . . . my kid brother," Sonny added for emphasis, grinning down sweetly at Amiq. Even though they were about the same age, Amiq was still nearly a head shorter than he was.

Amiq was starting to revive now, and Sonny half expected him to get mad about being called a kid—and by Sonny, too—but instead he just grinned up at the general with that big, goofy grin of his.

"Yes, sir," Amiq said. "Just waiting here for my big brother." He gave Sonny a look.

"Father Mullen gave us permission to write home," Sonny added, because it was the first thing that came into his mind. "Our mother . . ."

Suddenly Sonny didn't have the slightest idea what he should say about their mother.

"Our mother's not doing so well," Amiq said quick, starting to rev up like he always did in class discussions. "Her dog team took sick, and it's going to be a tough winter for them with all the dogs down and all."

He smiled real big, and Sonny had to turn away quick to keep from laughing. He stole a quick glance at the general. The general was frowning as though he were starting to catch on. Amiq's smile died, like he knew he'd gone too far.

"She traps," Sonny said quickly.

"She has to be able to run a trapline this time of year. It's critical, sir," Amiq added.

Critical? Where in the heck did that kid get his words? Sonny watched the general to see if this word surprised him, but the general just glanced at his watch like he wasn't even listening anymore.

"All right then, gentlemen," he said. "Well, it's nearly lunchtime now, isn't it?"

"Yes, sir," they both said brightly.

"Maybe we'll see you and your brother at lunch," the general told Sonny. Then he bent his head back into his papers and moved on.

As soon as the he was out of earshot, Amiq slumped back into the wall like all his muscles had melted. Then he looked Sonny square in the eye and smiled. Sonny'd never seen him smile a real smile like that. Not at him, anyhow.

"Let's split," Amiq said, and for a moment it seemed like they really were brothers.

Sonny thought briefly about lunch, lunch with the general.

Then he nodded his head and smiled. "That guy sure gives me the creeps," he said.

Amiq smiled, too. "No shit."

Without hardly thinking about it, Amiq took Sonny to that spot in the woods that looked like a little room made of trees, the one that Luke and Bunna had found. Their hideout. Sonny had never seen it before.

"How'd you find this place?" Sonny asked, looking around, clearly impressed.

Amiq smiled. "Luke and Bunna found it. Trying to hide from old man Pete." He thought of old man Pete's wrinkled-up face and the suspicious way he always looked at the Eskimo kids. "Man, that bugger's mean," he said.

Sonny grinned. "Never been mean to me," he said.

Amiq rolled his eyes. "Yeah, well, you tell him about this here Eskimo fort, and I'll have to kill ya," he said in his best John Wayne voice. "And if they find out I took you here, I may have to kill you anyhow," he added. "'Course, I do owe you something, us being brothers and all."

Sonny laughed. "Yeah. Practically twins."

Amiq was warming up to being out in the woods, out in their hideout, their Eskimo hideout, out here with an Indian, both of them hiding from the military. This was an adventure, all right, a real adventure.

"Ah well, you know how it is with these Na-tives," he said, pinching his voice up a notch. "They all of them look alike, and that there's a fact."

Now both of them were laughing, laughing about the general actually mistaking them for brothers. *Brothers!*

"Kid brother," Sonny snorted, patting Amiq sweetly on the head.

"No!" Amiq hollered gleefully. "No. Twins, remember? *Twins!*"

They were laughing really hard now.

"The whole dog team?" Sonny said. "The whole team took sick? All together?"

"Measles," Amiq said crisply, "Siberian measles."

Sonny doubled over. "Stop!" he begged. "My mom doesn't even *have* dogs."

"I am sorry to hear that, very sorry indeed," Amiq deadpanned. "Well, we just might have to resort to snowshoes this year, son."

He reached down and picked up a spruce branch, all rusty orange with dead needles.

"We always use snowshoes," Sonny said.

"Oh, yeah. I forgot."

Amiq rolled the branch back and forth between his palms, watching the river and thinking how funny it was that things could change all of a sudden, people changing with them.

"What about those tests?" Sonny said. "What were they?"

"Hell if I'm going to drink iodine-131," Amiq said.

"What's iodine-131?"

Amiq shrugged, running his finger along the rough edge of the spruce branch, making the dead needles shoot off like little arrows. "It ain't sacramental wine, that's for sure." He looked down, thinking about that name. *Iodine-131.* It sounded like a cross between some kind of medicine and some kind of motor oil.

"I grew up with scientists, and I'm sure as heck not going to be somebody's lab animal," Amiq said.

"You grew up with scientists?"

"You know, the Naval Arctic Research Laboratory. It's in Barrow. You never hear about it?"

Sonny shook his head.

"Yeah, well, I spent a lot of time there after my mom and brothers died. After the fire . . ."

Amiq looked down, bending the dead twig farther and farther back against itself, aware of the fact that Sonny was watching him. Not wanting to look up. Not wanting to say anything. What was there to say? He was surprised to hear himself talking about the fire like that, and talking about it with Sonny, of all people. He'd never said anything about the fire to anybody, but here was Sonny, sitting right next to him, nodding his head like he knew all about it—fires in the dead of winter when the stove is roaring hot and the house dry as tinder. A house so small it had only one tiny window in it.

"My mom. She pushed me out the window just before the roof fell," Amiq said. "I was the youngest, the only one who fit."

It felt like it was somebody else talking, somebody whose voice had become little more than a whisper, a whisper that seemed really loud in the silence that surrounded them. They sat there, the two of them, all alone in that silence. When the spruce twig in Amiq's hand snapped in half, it sounded like gunshot. Amiq took the two splinters of dead wood and stabbed them into the frozen ground.

"My dad died in the war," Sonny said.

Amiq looked up quick, but he didn't say a word.

"Left my mom alone with all us kids."

Amiq had known that Sonny didn't have a dad, but he'd never really thought about it. Now he realized something surprising: both he and Sonny knew what it felt like to grow up with only one parent—Sonny with his mom and all those brothers and sisters and him with nobody left but his old man.

"My old man was in the war, too. Ever since the fire, though, he likes his jug," Amiq said. "Likes his jug a whole lot."

He mounded up a little pile of dead leaves and needles around the bottom of one of the spruce twigs, wishing, suddenly, that he hadn't mentioned that part about his dad drinking. Him and his big mouth. He looked up quick, brushing the dirt from his hands and forcing himself to smile.

"Yeah, but you know what? Them scientists pay twenty-five cents apiece for lemmings, and they always have a hot meal. Beef stew and chicken soup, that kind of stuff. And they got a whole library full of books, science books, mostly. That's where I pretty much grew up, at that library. They're the ones paid to send me here, too. They figure I'm gonna come back home and be a scientist."

It felt like he was talking too fast.

"So are you?"

"Am I what?"

"Going to be a scientist?"

"Heck if I know. All I know for sure is they aren't going to turn me into some kind of lab animal. I seen what they do to lab animals."

Sonny fidgeted. "Least they pay your way home, summers," he offered.

Amiq looked at Sonny. "You can't ever go home summers?"

He didn't really have to ask. He knew it was true. But he'd never really thought about it.

"Mom's got a lot of other mouths to feed," Sonny said. "Guess I'm down for the count."

Sonny looked so sad all of a sudden that Amiq wanted to say something to make him laugh. He pinched his voice up tight again, just like how the general talked, like how generals in movies acted.

"An educated man we shall have," he said.

And Sonny did laugh. Both of them laughed softly, like two educated men. It was not the kind of laugh you laugh when something's really funny, though. It was more the kind you laugh when something bad happens and there's nothing left to do but laugh.

Sonny looked out across the river to where the last of the sun was sinking behind a bald-topped hill. It was glowing like the embers of a dying fire, and the shadows in Amiq's hideout had started to get dark and flickery. *Flickering in a funny way*, Sonny thought suddenly, just as the flickering began to sharpen into a small shaft of bright light. Without saying a word, both boys dropped down low on their bellies. Somebody who didn't know much about walking in the woods was making a lot of noise, cracking dead wood with every step, swinging a bright light every which way. Amiq and Sonny lay still as stones. Sonny could feel his heart pounding hard against the cold ground. He thought maybe he could feel Amiq's heart pounding just as hard, their two hearts pounding warnings back and forth through the hard dark earth. That flickering light, searching the woods, made him think of the crazy gleam Father Mullen got in his eyes when he got really mad.

They waited, without hardly breathing, until the light faded off into a distant pinpoint, then went out altogether, like a snuffed candle. Slowly they eased themselves back up, still afraid to even breathe.

"We better figure out a way to get back into the school or they gonna send the dogs out after us," Amiq whispered, finally.

Dogs? "What dogs?"

Amiq grinned. "Your mother's dead dogs."

Sonny punched him on the shoulder, hard, but that crazy Eskimo just kept on grinning that dumb old grin of his, the one that made you want to laugh out loud. That grin that made you think about making your own law, rather than following somebody else's.

"What the heck you get us into, Amundson?" Sonny said.

"What we got here, son, is a real honest ad-ven-shur."

"Yeah, well, we better come up with a way to get back in without getting caught, there, *cowboy*," Sonny said.

"Piece of cake," Amiq said. "Piece of cake."

Amiq was not the best stepladder—his shoulders were bony, and he swayed a bit under Sonny's weight. But even with all that weight on his shoulders, he was still acting like everything was easy, like everything would always be easy. He was going to push Sonny right up into the dorm window, and then Sonny was supposed to lean down and yank him up.

"It'll be a piece of cake," Amiq says.

Sonny doesn't think this is what you would call a brilliant plan, but he doesn't have a better one, and time is running out. He gazes down the length of the shadowy gray wall from his uncertain perch, his eyes wary.

"See," Amiq whispers, "all the windows are all dark. Everyone's at dinner."

"And why aren't we at dinner, again?" Sonny asks.

"The dogs," Amiq says. "The dead dogs."

Sonny grins at the thought of the dogs with their Siberian measles. "Somebody's gotta bury them," he says with a little laugh. But he knows what Amiq's really thinking. Amiq thinks they'll tell Father that they lost track of time doing homework. Now that one's really funny.

Amiq hangs on hard to Sonny's sharp ankles while Sonny tries to pull himself up and wiggle into the partially opened window. In the final moments, Amiq has to push up on Sonny's feet because Sonny is just too darn long to fold up easily into a space like that. But finally his feet flap into the window, fishlike.

Sonny glances sideways at the darkened hallway, and seeing no one, he pokes his head back out the window to give Amiq the all-clear sign. "Come on, hurry," he says, reaching down.

Amiq's arms are skinny but hard as birch saplings. His hands clamp onto Sonny's wrists, and he pulls harder and harder, walking his legs up the wall.

Now they're standing in the darkened space, the two of them together, feeling pretty proud of themselves, their laughter hushed but triumphant. Maybe it wasn't such a bad plan after all.

That's when they hear the voice hissing in the shadows. The sound of it makes their blood run cold.

"You boys think you're pretty smart, don't you."

Father Mullen.

Smart is not at all what they feel, following Mullen down the dimly lit halls, knowing they managed to pick the wrong time and the wrong window. Knowing it's a mistake that's going to cost them. Big-time.

And now Father is standing there in his office, telling them that evil has consumed them, spawns of Satan. His words seem to vibrate in the air around them, like a deadly swarm of black mosquitoes. Father is so angry that whole sentences are rattling in his throat, just waiting to get out. Like wasps. The sound is so terrible, all they can do is stand there, in the middle of it, watching the way Father fondles that two-by-four in the buzzing darkness. Swinging it from one hand to the other like an animal playing with its prey.

"Spare the rod . . ." Father rattles, swinging hard.

It stings like hell, that two-by-four, swinging back and forth, first to Amiq, then to Sonny, burning hot with every crack. Neither of them makes a sound, though—even when it feels like it's crushing bone—because it's the words Father says that sting worse than the blows. It's the sound of Father Mullen's voice, rasping like bees as he tells them both that they're nothing more than dirty little savages and there's no way in Hell either one of them could ever—*ever*—get into Heaven.

Nobody cares what happens to them except for Father, he hisses, because their people, their Native People, are as loose as rabbits with their kids.

Father is swinging that two-by-four back and forth like it's a hammer, and the pain bites harder with each swing as he sinks his words—sharp as nails—right into them. All of them are doomed to Hell, he says, nearly out of breath—*all of them*: Sonny and his uneducated heathen mother along with Amiq and his no-good, drunken dad.

Amiq's got a hard look on his face, and you can tell he's shut Father out and gone someplace else, someplace mean and angry. You can tell he's decided he wouldn't go to Heaven even if they gave him a gold pass for the place.

Sonny's thinking about his mom, who wouldn't be at all proud to see him now. His mother, sewing slippers for the general's wife, slippers with those tiny designs that make her eyes sting in the smoky light of the kerosene lamp. Sewing just to keep the general's wife's feet warm so the general can go about his business of giving numbered juice to the kids at Sacred Heart School. Sewing just so both boys can stand there in front of Father to find out there's no possible way Father will ever forgive them for being heathens, even if there were some reason they wanted Father's forgiveness, which right now, they do not.

Right now both Sonny and Amiq are determined as hell to be the meanest heathens ever, burrowing down into their own dark hides.

Waiting for their time to come.

PART III
When the Time Comes
1962–1963

Giant chunks of blue-green ice drift in the water around us,
alive with icy breath.
Along the shore, patches of gray-green tundra float off into the mist,
as distant as dreams.
When the flash of light comes, it's sharp as a punch,
brighter than any sun we've ever seen.
And then it's gone,
and it's just us, skimming across the smooth black sea,
silent as spirits,
pitching our tent in the midnight sun and eating duck soup until
our bellies get warm and we dare to ask:
"What about that light?"
Uncle looks down, his face lit like a dark sun in the glow of the fire.
"Light?"
And all we ever know about that light is that it's something we
aren't supposed
to talk about, aren't supposed to remember, but we do.
Maybe it was part of an old story, a story that starts
with a nuclear flash too bright to
believe, a flash that changes
everything.

Coupons and Bomb Shelters

DECEMBER 1962

CHICKIE

If somebody presses the button, the world is going to blow up, and that's a fact. The Russians have enough atomic bombs aimed at us to blow our side of the world right off the map, and we have enough bombs aimed at them to destroy their side, too. All it takes is for one person on one side to press the button. The button is red, and it doesn't matter who presses it first, because as soon as it gets pressed, the bombs will keep flying until the whole world is blown to smithereens.

This is true, and everybody knows it. We practice for the bomb in class by ducking under our desks and putting our heads between our knees, which if you ask me is stupid. What good would it do to have your head between your knees if a bomb blows you up?

Father Flanagan has brought an old magazine story to class with a big picture of an atomic missile on one page. Below that is a photo of President Kennedy, smiling, just like in the portrait we have of him that hangs in the hallway near the gym. Evelyn thinks President Kennedy is cute. That's Evelyn for you.

Father tells Junior to read.

Junior is not a loud reader, but I hear him say it clear: "I believe that this nation should commit itself to achieving the goal, before this decade is out, of landing a man on the moon and returning him safely to the Earth. . . ."

Junior looks up. "Father?" he says. But Father doesn't hear him. Father is looking right at me. "What do you think, Chickie? Will the president achieve his goal? Will we beat the Russians to the moon?"

"Alan Shepard already went up into space," I say. "We'll beat the Russians for sure."

Bunna, sitting right behind me, snorts. I turn around and glare at him. Who needs some stupid boy pig-snorting down their neck all the time? Father nods and looks at Bunna.

"Bunna?"

"It's too late, Father," Bunna says. "The Eskimos already beat everybody. There's an Iñupiaq shaman who went to the moon a long time ago." He leans forward when he says it, drawing out the words like he's trying to make sure I hear them.

"You know, when I was a boy growing up in Boston, my mother used to tell *me* stories about the man in the moon," Father says. "When you look at the moon, you can even see his face, can't you?"

Bunna looks at me and makes his eyes go *naku,* which makes him look even goofier than normal. I turn around. Boys are so stupid sometimes.

But I know about the Iñupiaq shaman who went to the moon. I heard Aaka Mae's brother tell about it one time. Swede says it's just a story, all right, but there are some things Swede does not understand.

"Of course, if President Kennedy succeeds, the man in the moon story will take on a new meaning, won't it?" Father says.

"If President Kennedy gets a man to the moon, that shaman's house will have an American flag on it," Bunna whispers. His words tickle the back of my neck and make me itch.

"Why do we need a man on the moon?" Evelyn asks.

"We gotta have somewhere to go after the bomb drops," Amiq says.

Evelyn looks bombstruck.

"What's wrong with bomb shelters?" Michael O'Shay asks.

Everything, I think. Bomb shelters give me the creeps.

Somewhere down south in the lower 48 there were two newlyweds who spent their entire honeymoon in a bomb shelter. We saw the pictures in *Life* magazine. President Kennedy has one, too, I heard. A great big bomb shelter for him and Jackie and Caroline and John-John.

That honeymoon bomb shelter was six feet wide and fourteen feet long, which is barely bigger than a coffin, and it was so hot, the newlyweds spent most of their honeymoon taking Noxzema sponge baths to cool off.

If there were any bomb shelters in Alaska, they wouldn't be hot at all; they'd be frozen solid, like ice cellars. I've been in ice cellars before, too. Some of them are big as houses, but I sure wouldn't want to live in one.

In fact, the idea of being buried alive in the earth makes me feel dizzy, like somebody big is sitting on my chest. I think I'd rather take my chances with the bomb.

"All right girls and boys, it's time for lunch," Father says.

Kids are shoving books into their desks, and Junior is looking at me. "They're still talking about blowing up bombs in Point Hope," he whispers.

Blowing up bombs in Point Hope? That's right next to Kotzebue!

"Look." He has a newspaper, a small one. The headline on the front page says "Project Chariot still on."

"What?"

"Project Chariot, that's what they call it. More bombs than at Hiroshima."

Junior is still whispering, and I don't know why. If it were me, I'd be hollering. But that's Junior for you.

"Father?" I say. But Father is already out the door.

Me, Evelyn, Rose, and Donna are in the library because we're supposed to do a paper on the race to the moon. Instead, we're listening to Evelyn read "Can This Marriage Be Saved?" from the *Ladies' Home Journal* and laughing at the way she reads it, her voice all high-pitched and girly-girly. Evelyn likes to read that kind of stuff because Evelyn is totally boy crazy. I'm not exactly sure when this happened, but if you ask me, it's boring.

Bunna's sitting one table over from us, trying to pretend

he's completely absorbed in some book, which is totally silly, because Bunna is not a reader. He might have the others fooled, but I am not fooled at all: Bunna is eavesdropping. He keeps glancing over at us sideways every few seconds, and whenever our eyes meet, he looks down quick at his book, trying to act like he doesn't see me, which makes me mad.

I pick up a copy of *Life* magazine and start flipping through it to hide the fact that Bunna is really bothering me.

"Okay, so now here's Jan's side of the story," Evelyn trills.

Bunna grins at his book in a way that makes me want to tell Evelyn to shut up, for crying out loud.

"I don't know why Bill always thinks I'm threatening to leave him," Evelyn reads, making her voice sound like she's about to cry. "I wish he'd understand that I need to take care of my mother, too. It doesn't mean I don't love him. My mother is 73 years old, and she needs my help, but Bill doesn't understand. He says it's either him or her. . . ."

"That doesn't even make sense," Rose says.

"You know how white people are," Evelyn says.

Then she looks at me and says, "Oops, sorry, Chickie."

I slug her hard anyhow, and Evelyn leans over toward Donna and says, "Help me Donna, I been attacked by a mean *White Woman*."

Bunna hunches down lower into his book, and you can tell he's trying hard not to laugh out loud. This makes me so mad, I want to walk right over there and punch him, too, but I restrain myself.

I'm beginning to blush, anyhow, so I grab that *Life*

magazine and start to study it page by page, ignoring stupid squawking Bunna as hard as I can. There's a double-paged spread of Elvis Presley, big as life, swaggering across the stage in a pair of tight white pants. I lay it out flat on the table, which works to change the subject, fast.

"Mmmmm," Rose sighs. "Elvis!"

"The way he moves his hips," Evelyn moans.

They have forgotten all about Bunna, sitting there next to us. Now he's looking as embarrassed as I was, which makes me smile.

"Sister Sarah says that's devil music," Donna says.

"Looks like an angel to me," Evelyn says.

Rose says, "Every boy looks like an angel to you, Evelyn."

Evelyn smiles. "Elvis, he got Indian blood. Bet you didn't know that."

"Oooooh, Evie," I say, rolling my voice for Bunna's benefit. "Could be he's your *cousin*."

"Kissing cousins, maybe." Evelyn raises her eyebrows in a way that makes it look like she's saying certain things without actually saying them.

"Eeew! That's yucky," I say, slapping the magazine shut. Why does Evelyn always have to find a way to talk about boys and kissing? And other things.

On the back cover of *Life* magazine there's a picture of a pink convertible filled with big-chested blond girls in shorts. The one sitting up on the trunk of the car is holding a big armload of Betty Crocker cake mixes.

"I want one of those," Evelyn says.

She's talking about the car, of course.

"You want everything," I say.

Then I notice the small print under that picture. I lean down close and read it. "Hey, did you know you can earn a car with Betty Crocker coupons?"

Out of the side of my eye, I see Bunna straighten up suddenly.

"What's Betty Crocker coupons?" Rose asks.

"They're on the tops of the cake boxes," Bunna says.

Evelyn scowls at Bunna.

"How many coupons?" Rose asks.

How in the heck does Bunna know about cake coupons? That's what *I* want to ask.

"I think it says fifty thousand," I say. I have to squint hard at the small print, because I'm not wearing my new glasses. I'm not wearing my glasses because I think I look more sophisticated without them, and a person with freckles needs all the sophistication she can get.

"If you could afford to buy fifty thousand cake mixes, you wouldn't need to pay for a car with coupons," Evelyn says. Then she gives Bunna a look—an Indian warrior look.

"C'mon girls," she says. "Let's *go*."

It was Bunna's idea, all right, but Junior wrote it down. That's when we discovered that Junior knew how to write a really good letter. It was Father Flanagan who made it happen, of course. Father started making plans the minute Bunna burst into class.

"Look here, Father, look at this!" Bunna is practically hollering, waving the letter like a white flag.

Father takes it and reads slowly, nodding his head. Then he looks at the picture of the blond girls with the cake boxes. By the time he's done looking back and forth from one to the other, he's smiling.

"This project would take a lot of work," he says. "And we'll need some students with first-rate penmanship."

I raise my hand right away. "I have great penmanship, Father," I say. I'm not bragging. It's true, and everybody knows it.

"So do I," Bunna says.

Everyone laughs, of course, because everyone knows that Bunna's handwriting is a train wreck.

But in the end we all wrote letters, good penmanship or no penmanship. We each wrote hundreds of letters, copying the same words over and over:

DEAR MRS.———————,
I AM A STUDENT AT SACRED HEART SCHOOL,
A PAROCHIAL BOARDING SCHOOL SITUATED
IN THE HEART OF ALASKA. MOST OF THE
STUDENTS HERE ARE NATIVE ALASKAN, AND
MANY OF US HAD NEVER BEEN OUTSIDE OUR
HOME VILLAGES PRIOR TO COMING TO SACRED
HEART. OUR SCHOOL, SACRED HEART, IS RUN
BY THE GENEROUS DONATIONS OF GOD-FEARING
CITIZENS LIKE YOURSELF. WE ARE CURRENTLY
IN DESPERATE NEED OF A BUS TO ENABLE
US TO ENJOY THE LEARNING OPPORTUNITIES
AND SPORTS ACTIVITIES AVAILABLE TO US

THROUGHOUT OUR REGION. WE HAVE DISCOVERED
THAT IF WE SAVE UP ENOUGH BETTY CROCKER
COUPONS, WE CAN EARN A BUS FOR OUR SCHOOL.
WE HOPE THAT YOU WILL BE WILLING TO SAVE
COUPONS FOR US. . . .
SINCERELY,

———————————, SACRED HEART STUDENT

We wrote about 5,000 of those letters, sitting there in the library every day before dinner, writing and writing. Me and Bunna sat next to each other and got into some sort of unspoken competition over it. I was faster than he was, which gave me endless satisfaction.

Sister's the one who makes me late to the library one day— she needed help in the laundry. But it's Amiq, of course, who has to make an issue of it. He starts yapping the second I slide into my chair.

"Look here, Snowbird. Bunna's winning," he says.

I grab a piece of paper and start writing as fast as I can, slowly realizing that something is going on, something I can't deny.

Bunna isn't writing. He isn't writing one little bit: he's watching me and he isn't even trying to hide it. I can see him, out of the side of my eye, just staring. I look up, very firmly, look him square in the eye. I figure I'm going to stare him down and make him feel about two feet tall, but he just grins right back at me, tall as ever.

"Where were you?" he says.

Where was I? All of a sudden, I feel this fluttering feeling in my stomach—I swear, just like in the songs—and just as suddenly I notice Bunna's eyes. Bunna has these really, really soft brown eyes, the kind that make you feel warm and happy when you look into them. Chocolatey brown. His eyes are a sweet, chocolatey brown. I notice them for the first time right then and there—and can't for the life of me imagine how I failed to notice them before. All of a sudden I just have to stand up, quick, because two things have just occurred to me, two things that surprise me right down to the very tips of my toes: 1) Bunna likes me, and 2) This does not bother me, not one little bit.

"Laundry!" I blurt it out without even thinking. "I was doing laundry." Then I get up and just about run out of that room. I go as fast as I can, because Amiq is sprawled out at the table by the door, watching us, and I just know he's going to say something to embarrass me, which he does.

"Hey, Snowbird. You're blushing," he says.

"Too much hot air in this place!" I snap, marching off with as much dignity as I can manage.

I hear Bunna laughing behind me, but I don't mind at all because it's a warm laugh, and I'm already out in the hall. And by now, I'm practically laughing, too.

Even though there's no one here to see me, I am smiling all the way down the hall, every step of the way, right past the cafeteria, past the gym and past the portrait of President Kennedy, who is smiling, too. Like he just touched the moon.

Our Uncle's Gun
JUNE 6, 1963

LUKE

The dream ebbs away like water melting into sand, but even with his eyes wide open, Luke feels the pain. It was a dream of bright flashes and shadowy shapes and the kind of hurt that makes it hard to breathe, like something bad is happening. Something very bad, with people knowing what it is but not saying, refusing to even look at you. The kind of dream that feels significant—more substantial than the army cot or the sunny window or the smell of the hair grease that Bunna is combing into his hair, like an artist applying paint to a canvas.

Today is the day they're going home for summer break, and the air is thick with anticipation.

Bunna stands before the mirror, examining his hair with a look of satisfaction.

"I had this dream," Luke says to Bunna's back. But suddenly the dream details get all mixed up, and the words forming themselves in Luke's mouth don't make any sense.

"Mmm?" says Bunna, turning sideways to examine the side of his neck in the mirror.

"We were living in an ice cellar," Luke says. But he isn't sure who he means by *we*—not him and Bunna alone—and he doesn't think *ice cellar* is the right word, either. The right word is an Iñupiaq word, trapped in between his tongue and his teeth. Voiceless.

"Hope Uncle's ice cellar is full of *maktak*," Bunna says, regarding his reflection sideways. "That's the first place I'm going when we get home."

Suddenly something inside Luke snaps into clarity. Something important.

"We're not going home," he says, swinging his legs over the side of the bed and standing up. "We're staying here."

Because all of a sudden Luke knows with absolute certainty that he and Bunna can't go home. He doesn't know how or why he knows this, he just does. They've been planning to go home forever and can't wait to get there, but now there's something inside him that says they can't go. The dream. It came from the dream, somehow. Even if the plane flew down to Sacred Heart School and landed right outside their window, singing their names like rock songs, they could not go. This is what Luke suddenly knows.

"*What?*"

Bunna has turned around and is now staring at Luke, dumbstruck.

"We aren't going anywhere. We're staying here."

"Like hell!" Bunna turns away again and starts shoving

things into his duffle bag.

Luke scowls out at the birch tree, trying to ignore him, which is impossible because Bunna is wadding up stray socks and shorts and punching them into his duffle with a force so fierce even the birch tree seems to feel it, tapping its black branch against the window like a warning.

Luke looks at the gun on the wall—the one Uncle Joe gave him—and all he wants to do, right now, is go home. He wants this so bad it takes his breath away.

Bunna snaps his duffle shut, his eyes following Luke's. Then he reaches for the gun.

"You aren't taking that gun," Luke says. His voice feels cold and steely.

Suddenly the gun is the most important thing in the world.

Bunna scowls. "Uncle Joe says you gotta bring it home for summer."

"I'm not going home this summer."

Bunna pulls the gun closer. "Yeah, well, I am."

Luke takes a step forward. Just one step. Even though they're about the same height, Luke's shoulders are broader than Bunna's.

"Not with my gun," he says. He wants, desperately, to say something else, something powerful. He isn't sure what—he only knows for certain that it has nothing to do with the gun. Nothing at all.

"I'm listening to Uncle Joe, not you," Bunna says, setting the gun down by his duffle like a dare, like he's daring Luke to do something. Luke wants to do something, all right. He wants to do something real bad.

"You're not listening to what I'm saying." The words taste like tough old meat. He tears them off with his teeth, strand by strand. "You're. Just. Being. Stupid."

"I'm not stupid. What the heck you wanna stay at this stupid place for when you could be home hunting with Uncle? *Stupid!*"

"Quit being a damn baby."

Luke wanted to say something stronger, something that would shake Bunna awake. Maybe the words he needed were Iñupiaq words, and maybe he had spoken English so long he no longer knew them. Or maybe there were just some things words couldn't say. Things nobody could say.

"We could make money this summer," he says. "Go to Fairbanks like Amiq . . ."

Amiq was going to have a job in Fairbanks this summer, live with a family—they could, too, Luke thinks, him and Bunna.

"Forget it," Bunna snaps.

"Grow up, man, it's—"

"Forget it!" Bunna's mouth is like some kind of slingshot, shooting rock-hard words. *Bing, bing, bing.* And his ears seem plugged shut with those same rocks.

More than anything, Luke wants to shake him, shake the rocks right out of his head. Shake and shake and shake.

"Why don't you just—" His voice rises perilously.

"Forget it!" Bunna barks.

"Hell, if you can't even—"

"FORGET IT!"

"LISTEN!" Luke hollers, using the side of his fist to open Bunna's ears, shoving him right up against the bed, slamming him hard. Shoving him into the wall. "Damn it! What's the matter with you?" Luke's been gritting his teeth so hard, his jaw aches. "We could make some money, staying here!"

He slams Bunna into the wall with a perfect uppercut, trying to follow the rules, just like Father Mullen taught them, but suddenly both of them are on the floor, lunging at each other's throats, not following any rules to any game either of them ever played. Making for themselves a new game, dangerous as thin ice.

And Bunna's strong, too—as strong as Luke, maybe even stronger. But Luke weighs more, and he has Bunna pinned against the floor, pinned hard enough to leave marks. Glaring down at him. Bunna glares right back, without a sound. Fierce as a wolverine. Fierce and a little desperate, Luke realizes suddenly. *Like an animal caught in a trap.* The thought scares him.

"Look," he says, letting up, "it just don't feel right, us going home this time. Okay? Something's not right. It's just a feeling I have."

Bunna looks at him. All of a sudden he understands what Luke is trying to say—you can see it in his eyes—but there's nothing he can do about it. You can see that, too.

"I gotta go home." He says it so slow and low, it sounds like each word is sucking the breath right out of him.

"I just . . . have to."

Luke has no choice: he has to let go. There isn't anything more he can do. He sees it in Bunna's eyes. Bunna is going home because he has to, and Luke isn't because he can't. And all because of a bunch of dumb feelings nobody in their right mind would want to feel.

They'd never ever been apart before. This thought hits Luke like lightning. In their whole lives, they've never spent a single day apart.

Bunna stands up, rubbing his shoulder. Luke stands up, too, scared and confused. The whole world is spinning out of control, like a wounded animal running, and there is nothing left to hold onto. Nothing except that gun, standing next to Bunna. *Uncle Joe's gun.*

"You're not taking the gun."

Bunna shoves it at him. "So keep it."

And then they just stand there, the gun in between the two of them like the ghost of the fight, still beating in their hearts. And there is nothing else to be said.

Nothing at all.

Eskimo Kiss

JUNE 7, 1963

CHICKIE

We earned enough Betty Crocker coupons for a new bus, but it was time for summer vacation, and the bus wouldn't come until fall, so we had to ride the old military bus one more time, all the way to Fairbanks. Bunna was going home for the summer, but Luke wasn't, which was weird. Those two are like Mutt and Jeff, and I couldn't figure out why Luke would stay at school when Bunna wasn't going to. Or why Bunna would go when Luke was staying.

I climbed up into the bus and sat down on a squeaky seat by a window on the school side, watching everybody file in. Donna and Sonny stood outside by the wall, watching us. They weren't going home either, and they looked really small and lonely, standing there all by themselves. Bunna climbed onboard and sat down right smack in front of me, staring out the window at Sonny and Donna, only he wasn't really looking at them, I could tell. He was staring at the spot right next to them, where Luke should have been but wasn't—an empty stretch of wall, gray as smoke. Bunna glared at that spot like he was trying to ignite it with his eyes, staring so hard I bet he didn't see the flicker of movement in one of the windows of the boys' dorm, didn't even see Luke's face hover there for just a second.

Rose and Evelyn came bursting out of the door, late as usual. Rose was dragging a duffle almost as big as she was, and Sonny grabbed it from her like he was John Wayne or something.

Then, before anybody knew what had happened, there was Luke, marching toward the bus with his gun at his side, the barrel pointed down. He was frowning—not looking at anyone in particular—just frowning at everyone and everything, I guess. He walked over to the back of the bus, where all the luggage was stacked, and slid that gun right in on top of all the duffle bags, very carefully. We all were watching him, but nobody said a thing.

I turned around, without even thinking about it, to see Bunna's reaction. But at the exact same moment I turned, Bunna leaned his head over the seat, and we collided midturn, his nose against my cheek. He hollered "*Ow*," and I turned beet red.

"Ooo," said Evelyn, "Eskimo kiss," and everyone laughed. Everyone but me and Bunna.

Stupid Evelyn.

I stared straight out the side window, burning with embarrassment. Not wanting to face anyone.

Luke was walking back into the school real slow, and I envied the way he walked, so straight and sure, like he didn't give a fiddle what anyone thought. He never looked back. Not once.

When Father Flanagan turned the key in the ignition and let up on the brake and that old bus started to creak along on its rusty gears, Bunna turned to look out the window, quick, looking back at the school like he expected to see Luke come running after us. But Luke was gone, and in half a breath, so were we.

I just sat there, one hand clutching the other, still feeling embarrassed. Michael O'Shay was sitting all alone, directly across from me, and he kept looking at me like he thought we should feel some special kind of bond, us both being white; like maybe we're family or something, which we most certainly were not.

"Where you from, again?" he asked.

"Kotzebue," I told him. We'd had this conversation before, the two of us. Which Michael O'Shay should have remembered. But Michael O'Shay was from Fairbanks, and he was under the impression that the whole state, with the possible exception of Anchorage, was just some sort of big shadow Fairbanks made.

"I mean where are you *really* from?" he said, like Kotzebue was just some sort of excuse I always made.

"Kotzebue," I said, turning away from him to watch the Sacred Heart trees sweeping by the window.

"But where's your family from?" he persisted.

"Where's *yours* from?"

"Fairbanks," he said. "First generation."

All of a sudden Bunna turned around, glaring. "What the heck's that supposed to mean?" Bunna said. But he was looking at me when he said it, not O'Shay. And he was looking with a protective sort of look, too, looking me right straight in the eye. I looked right back, very glad for the fact that it was starting to get dark and nobody could see me blush. Michael O'Shay never said another word.

When Father stopped for gas, I got off the bus and went over to the edge of the woods and just stood there, breathing in all the warm, starry darkness. And I don't mean the air was warm, because it wasn't. The warmth came from someplace inside me, someplace so deep and private, it made me feel like I was sparkling, too.

"You like that guy?"

Bunna's voice came out of nowhere, and his words were just as surprising. He had walked over, away from the others, and now he was standing right next to me. His voice made his words sound more like an accusation than a question.

I was so surprised I said, "What guy?" which was a dumb thing to say because I knew perfectly well who he was talking about.

"O'Shay."

Did I like O'Shay? Skinny know-it-all Michael O'Shay? "No. I don't like him."

I guess I was supposed to say something else, something smart and funny, but everything smart and funny dried up in my mouth with surprise. Bunna was jealous!

All of a sudden it felt like I'd grown extra limbs and didn't know what to do with them. I shoved my hands into my pockets and stared up at the night sky. It was like I was seeing it for the first time ever. There were so many stars! Where did they all come from?

Bunna was watching them, too, now.

"What do you call that one, the one with the three stars right there in a row?" he said.

"Orion's Belt," I said. Swede taught me that one ages ago.

"*Tuvaurat*," Bunna said softly. "That's three hunters, returning from caribou hunting." He waved his arms off vaguely into the direction where those star hunters might have been hunting. "See the horns over there?"

All of a sudden I did. I really did. A pile of horns. And before I even knew what was happening, Bunna leaned down close and kissed me. Kissed me right there on the edge of the sparkling black woods halfway to Fairbanks, beneath stars that looked like caribou horns. And I kissed him back, too, kissed him for a long, long time.

Bunna's lips were soft and warm, and he smelled like Palmolive soap and laundry detergent and hair grease, and right then and there I decided that mixture of Palmolive soap, laundry detergent, and hair grease was probably the best smell in the whole wide world.

Eskimo kiss, I thought, and that thought made me smile, walking back to the bus with Bunna, our arms touching in a way that felt totally natural, like it was the way things were supposed to be.

"Next year we gonna have a new bus," Bunna said as he slid into the seat beside me. He was talking to Michael O'Shay, like it was some kind of challenge, but Michael didn't respond—he just stared out the window into the darkness. "And that bus is gonna have real soft seats, too," he whispered to me.

But I didn't care anything at all about our new bus anymore. And I didn't care about the old one, either, bouncing along in its rickety old way. All I cared about was Bunna's hand holding mine, our fingers lacing together, back and forth, learning a new language all the way to Fairbanks. It was a language about love—holding on and letting go, holding on and letting go.

Forever

LUKE

We used to watch movies in the community center in the summer, sometimes. The ones with Roy Rogers and John Wayne and all those cowboys. Bunna liked Roy Rogers best, but me, I liked the rodeo. I liked the way those cowboys came shooting out on their bucking broncos, hanging on for dear life and never letting go, no matter what, waving and smiling at the crowd. Those broncos tossed them up and down and waved them back and forth like flags, but they never let go.

Tough, them guys.

In the summers back home, me and Bunna and Isaac used to play along the beach late at night. We always got to go boating, sometimes, with Uncle Joe or one of the others, staying out there all night long, watching the midnight sun circle the sky, slung low on the horizon late and rising up toward the middle near dawn.

Now Isaac's gone for good, which nobody talks about, and

Bunna's gone for the summer, which I don't want to think about. So it's just me and Sonny and Donna, eating dinner all alone in the big, echoing Sacred Heart cafeteria, with the sun making long dark shadows and me knowing, all of a sudden. Just knowing.

Some people could know things before they happen without even thinking about them, and I wish to heck I wasn't one of those people, because what I know right now has to do with the way Sister Mary Kate and Father Flanagan are standing there at the door to the cafeteria, their heads bowed, watching me while they talk. Talking about me and about the news they don't want to tell me, the news I don't want to hear. I can feel it. Heck, anybody could feel it, because right now the whole room is heavy as cement with it.

I remember the dream I had, all of a sudden, in one bright flash. Was it last night? Last week? Last year? My mind feels like it's stepped out of time into a place where everything is foggy. Everything except the dream: it's old Uiñiq, clear as day, making arrows like he always used to when we were kids. Little kid arrows for me and Bunna, and we're running along the beach, chasing birds late into the summer night. And every time we break an arrow, there's a new one already made.

In my dream, Uiñiq is giving Bunna one last arrow, but when he sees me, he shakes his head slowly, and there's a look on his face that chills me right through to the bone. Bunna has his back to me, too, and he won't turn around. He knows I'm right there, all right, but he won't turn. It's like a door shutting—Uiñiq with his last arrow and Bunna with his back turned. A door closed forever.

Suddenly I'm aware of Sister, still standing in the doorway to the cafeteria, still watching.

"There's been an accident," Sister's going to say. Or maybe she doesn't say it at all. Maybe she doesn't even have to say it because I already know.

I know already.

Old Uiñiq is long dead, and now Bunna is with him.

I already know this. I know it now like I knew it a second ago, like I knew it last week. All of time—past and present and even future, all of it running together in my head like the gravy on my plate.

That's what I will remember, I'm thinking, realizing it's a crazy thought even as I think it: I will remember the gravy on my plate, running into the potatoes and peas with Father Flanagan and Sister Mary Kate standing by that door over there, watching me, and me refusing to even look at them, just like Bunna refused to look at me. And Uiñiq shaking his head and scowling and me staring down at the gravy on my plate like there's gotta be some meaning there. Knowing there isn't.

That's what I'll remember.

"The plane didn't make it through the mountains," Father is saying. Or maybe he isn't really saying it. Maybe I just know that's what he's gonna say as I stand there in the door to the cafeteria not wanting to be there—not wanting to be anywhere.

There were a lot of other boarding-school kids on board

that plane, but only one of them was from Sacred Heart School, and only one of them was my brother.

Father and Sister stand with their shoulders sloped together, almost touching, and I stand right next to them, all alone, my shoulders square as rulers, not touching anything, pushing right past them before they can even reach out, pushing right out of the building, out into the woods. Away.

I have to get away from what I already know, from what I don't ever want to have to know: *my brother Bunna is dead.*

They don't even have to say it. I can feel it in the slope of their shoulders, in the air itself, in the way my chest gets tight like a cage that won't let me ever breathe deep again. I can feel Bunna's absence like you feel a part of you that's no longer there—a leg amputated, a lung gone.

Bunna is dead.

I'm running through the woods, deep into the trees, where there are no trails. No way in. No way out. It's getting dark, and I'm running blind. Maybe I'm running backward, watching the past wind away from me like a ruined film of Roy Rogers and John Wayne spilling out of a projector onto a dusty floor in a dark, empty room.

Gone.

Or maybe I'm not even running at all, not even moving, just standing there, letting spruce branches slap me in the face, slash my skin raw. It's a better kind of pain than the one I feel inside right now.

Inside there's only one thing I know: I have to get away

from everyone and everything because I'm like a dog with pain and I don't want nobody talking at me about it. I don't want nobody being sorry at me or following after me with some crap about the compassion of Christ. I just want to run and keep on running. Let them try to catch me. They can't. They can't because my pain's taking me places no one else can go. Places I gotta go all alone. Without Bunna. Me and Bunna who never in our whole lives have been apart. Not once. Me and Bunna who were spliced together from the day he was born, sliced apart forever now. Forever.

Nieces and nephews too numerous to count. That's what they always put on peoples' funeral papers, the ones they make at church. Funerals at the church back home are always packed full of people—nieces and nephews too numerous to count. But not here at Sacred Heart School, where there's no one to count family, no one counting me as left behind. No mom, no dad, no aunts, no uncles. *No brothers.*

I'm not running anymore, but my heart is banging at my ribs like a rabid fox. A fox locked up in a too-tight cage.

No brothers at all.

All of a sudden, anger washes over me in icy waves, making me clench my fists again and again, my worthless fists. I wanna beat the shit out of Bunna once and for all, but he's not there. I want to box him up so bad, he's gonna refuse to ever leave me. Then I'm crying, remembering how the last night we were together, that's just exactly what I did do. Beat the shit out of him until he stopped me with those words, those stupid words: "I gotta go home," he said. What in the hell does *home* mean to him now? To me without a brother? To anybody?

It's hot and sticky in the middle of all these Sacred Heart trees, and there isn't a drop of wind anywhere. I'm itching like crazy from spruce prickles and mosquito bites.

Back home there's a breeze coming in off the ocean ice, and I wish I could feel its cool breath on my sweaty neck right now. Wish I was sitting in a boat with chunks of ocean ice just sort of hanging there in between the smooth water and the cloudless sky—drifting with their reflections white and ghost-like against the glassy water.

I've got my eyes closed, imagining it, but when I open them, it's like the terror of a nightmare, looking into the darkness of Sacred Heart, trees blotting out everything.

Gone. Everything's gone.

Suddenly I realize I'm crying, crying so hard I can hardly breathe.

How can anybody even breathe in a place where there is no wind, no open sky, no ocean, no family? Nothing worth counting?

Ever.

PART IV
The Earth Can't Shake Us
1963–1964

---

*We
were here.
We were always here,
hanging on where others couldn't,
marking signs the others wouldn't,
counting kin our own way. We
survived. The earth
can't shake
us.*

He's My Brother
SEPTEMBER 1963

CHICKIE

When he came to pick us up in Fairbanks at the end of the summer, Father Flanagan was driving the new bus. But Bunna wasn't on it. Bunna would never ever sit next to me on the bus again, old or new. I'd spent so much time refusing to believe the truth of this that I felt totally numb inside, all hollowed out like that old, dead piece of military trash of a bus we weren't going to ride anymore. Only thing was, I wanted to ride it. I wanted to get on that old bus and let it bounce everything to pieces. Shake things back to normal again. I did not want to have to *remember* Bunna. But I didn't want to worry about forgetting him, either.

I was carrying my diary in my lap like an old assignment book with an assignment I couldn't let go of. I wanted to read and reread every word I'd ever written about Bunna. As I leafed though the book, the first words I ever wrote about him jumped off the page:

<u>BUNNA A IS A DUMB ANIMAL!!</u>

I was so mad when I wrote it that I pressed really hard and made little ridges on the paper. Now the words stand out on that page like Braille.

How can that be? That's what I want to know. Those words are still alive, but Bunna's dead. How can a dumb old piece of paper with a girl's silly writing outlive a boy with chocolatey brown eyes and a smile to die for?

It seemed like I was the only one on that whole bus thinking about Bunna. Everyone else was too excited about the new bus. *Bunna's bus!* Part of me wanted to scream it out, and part of me wanted to hoard his memory to myself and totally ignore the bus. And another part wanted to blame the bus for everything, which didn't make any sense at all.

We drove into the school grounds in full glory, Father honking the horn like he was the leader of a one-horned band. Before we had even properly stopped, Amiq, who had spent the summer working in Fairbanks, jumped off, Eskimo dancing—stomping his foot and waving one arm at that big expanse of shiny new bus like he'd just invented it and had made up a brand-new dance to tell the story.

The whole world could fall apart, and some things, like Amiq, would never ever change. That made me feel better and worse, both at the same time.

I could see Donna, Sonny, and the nuns standing by the door to the school, watching Amiq dance his bus dance. By this time Sister Mary Kate was so excited, she was practically dancing herself. I could hear her yelling right through the window of the bus. "Will you just look at that! It's a miracle, a complete miracle!"

You probably could have heard her yelling all the way to Fairbanks. That's how excited she was. She turned to Sister Sarah and hollered even louder, on account of Sister's hearing, "IT IS A MIRACLE, ISN'T IT, SISTER?"

Sister Sarah just scowled. She didn't like all the racket any more than I did, but Father Flanagan kept right on honking, and the kids kept leaping off the bus with big smiles like they were rock stars on tour or something. I guess I should have been glad about the fact that Father Mullen wasn't there to spread doom and gloom, like he always did. But I wasn't. I didn't care about any of it.

By the time it was my turn to climb down those new stairs, it felt like the din had turned my insides to mush and made my knees get as wobbly as day-old noodles. All I wanted to do was disappear.

That's when I saw Luke. He was standing way off to the side, like he wanted to disappear, too. When I looked at him, it felt like everyone else just melted away, and it was just us two, all alone, missing Bunna, together. I could tell, right then and there, that he knew about me and Bunna and how we'd kissed on the edge of the endless woods. I don't know how he knew, but he did. I guess that's how brothers are sometimes.

I don't know if I imagined it or not, the sudden silence that came right then. My ears rang with it.

Luke took one little step toward me. It was a tentative

sort of step, like he was trying to remember how to walk. And before I could even think about what I was doing, I dropped my duffle and started running toward him, sobbing and sobbing until there weren't any tears left inside me. Luke was crying, too, only you wouldn't have hardly been able to tell it. He just stood there, as rooted as a tree, tears running down his cheeks like they'd always been there. Like he'd been born in tears. Then he wiped his face with the sleeve of his shirt, grabbed my duffle, and we walked into the school together.

We didn't try to make our steps match, but they did match, perfectly. When we reached the door and I turned around to look back at the bus, I realized that all the others were just standing there, watching us. Most of the girls were crying, too, and Sister Mary Kate held her hand to her chest.

That big bus just sat there behind us all, shiny as shit.

"Damn bus," I muttered.

It was the first time in my life I ever swore out loud.

Luke took me to his secret place, his and Bunna's, and he made a big deal about how nobody was supposed to know about it, so I never told him that I already knew. I'd seen the two of them sneaking off and had followed them to see if I could get some ammunition to use against Bunna. I'd gotten so sick of Bunna teasing me, calling me Snowbird—I got my ammunition, too, all right. It came in the form of Bunna's toy gun, hidden in a box in their secret hideout. Bunna was too big to play with toy guns, and when I started calling him Roy Rogers, he quit calling me Snowbird. That's how ten-year-olds deal with stuff. Right before they turn into teenagers and learn how to kiss instead.

Sister Mary Kate kept telling us that God had called Bunna home early for a special reason. So when Luke took me to their secret hideout, I asked him about it.

"Do you believe that God called Bunna home for a special reason?"

"No," Luke said.

There was no way I could hide how bad it made me feel to hear him say that.

"I believe like Iñupiaqs believe," he said real quick, watching me.

I didn't say anything. I was afraid I'd start crying all over again.

"After a person dies, you gotta name a baby after them," he said. "The baby is the spirit of that person coming back. That's how you bring them back alive. With the name."

"Do you believe that?" I asked.

He shrugged. "Yeah."

"With Bunna? You believe it with Bunna?" I had to know.

Luke stared out at the river like he never even heard me. His face was hard and dark and still, like a stone in the bottom of a moving river.

"I never seen it yet with Bunna, but that's how it works," he said finally. "People say that, you know? They tell us how we're just like the ones we're named for. Like me. My *aaka* says

I walk the same way the one I was named after used to walk. Exact same way."

I looked at him, trying to imagine something about his walk a person might identify as someone else's. "I don't know about that," I said. "Guess I don't have that kind of name."

Luke smiled all of a sudden. "Yeah, but you know what they say about snowbirds, right?"

"You aren't supposed to mess with them?" I gave Luke a don't-mess-with-me kind of look.

Aaka Mae used to chase after boys who tried to hunt snowbirds, chase them with a broom, and if you were one of those boys you better hope she didn't catch you.

"The old women call them God's messengers," Luke said.

I smiled then, because this idea made me happy. But Luke wasn't looking at me. He was thinking hard about something else, something serious.

"I never eat *uunaalik* for a long time," he said finally.

I didn't know what *uunaalik* was and couldn't figure what eating it had to do with snowbirds. Or with Bunna. But I didn't say anything. I just looked up at the birch leaves and watched the way they flickered in the sunlight.

"That's whale meat and blubber, cooked," Luke said. "*Uunaalik*—the only time we get to eat it is right after they catch a whale. After they freeze the *maktak,* they can't cook it that way anymore."

He was fiddling with Bunna's toy gun, and I knew better than to say anything. I didn't have a clue why he wanted to talk about cooked blubber all of a sudden, but with Luke you just have to wait sometimes. He'll explain things, eventually. That's how he is.

"I haven't been home for spring whaling in nearly three years," he said at last. "When it comes to whaling, I'm only about 11 years old. That's how old I was last time I tasted *uunaalik*."

He sat there, just playing with that little tin gun, pulling the trigger back and forth so hard, it seemed like he was about to break it. Like he didn't even notice what he was doing. When he finally let go of the trigger, the gun made a sharp little clicking sound.

"The snowbirds come in the spring, right before whaling, so when you see the first snowbird, you know right away the whales are coming. That's why they call them God's messengers," he said.

The way he said the word *messengers* made it sound serious, but I looked up at him, smiling, because a funny idea had just popped into my head.

"Three whole years," I said, "and all you get here is a girl named Snowbird who can't even fly."

Luke tossed Bunna's gun back into the box and laughed for real, which I don't think he'd done in a long time.

"Nothing wrong with that," he said. "Could be worse. Could be a lot worse."

I looked at Luke, and a strange thought came into my head: *he's my brother now.* And it didn't have anything to do with Bunna, either. That was the strange part. Maybe nobody else would have understood it—him with pitch-black hair and me as light as snow—but to me it was as sure as the morning sunshine, brand new and old, both at the same time.

"My brother Isaac," Luke said suddenly, like he'd heard me thinking about brothers. "I have to find him."

Eskimo Rodeo

NOVEMBER 22, 1963

LUKE

I walk into the cafeteria feeling pretty good that day even though I'm late. It's Friday, so it's fish day. I like Fridays, and I like fish, too. The fish isn't frozen and juicy with seal oil, like the way we eat it back home—it's baked and gooey, but I still like it. And I especially like the cornbread they serve for breakfast on Fridays. It tastes great, smothered in butter and syrup.

Today, though, something's different. I feel it the minute I walk in. Something bad has happened. Again. Even if I can't feel it in my gut, the way I felt Bunna, I can tell right away, because nobody's smiling. Sister Mary Kate is serving slabs of cornbread like she doesn't even know it's food, her eyes red-rimmed and puffy.

Then I hear it—the sound of everybody talking about the news, most of them whispering like they're in church: President John F. Kennedy has just been shot. I suck in a big breath of sticky sweet air and sit down to eat. The cornbread turns into hard globs on our plates while we listen to the crackly sound of the radio. Reporters are talking about how President Kennedy got shot in the head and collapsed into his wife's arms in a car in Dallas, Texas. It's like being right there, the way they talk on the radio. We listen as they rush him to the hospital and talk about what's happening as it happens. At first they don't seem to know much. It's just the same voices saying the same things, over and over, like that's all there is.

Then we hear a man's voice, lone and final. "Ladies and gentlemen, the president is dead. The president, ladies and gentlemen, is dead at Parkland Hospital in Dallas."

It hits me in the chest with a dull thud, and I am feeling Bunna's dying again.

"How can this be?" Sister keeps saying again and again. "Oh Lord, how can this be?"

She says it over and over like a broken record until I want to tell her to stop. *Just stop.* But my throat is frozen.

"Our own president, our own Catholic president," Chickie blubbers. "Our very first one."

She's thinking of Bunna, too, I think.

Everybody else is hardly moving, just sitting there on narrow benches listening to the radio tell us how at this very moment, right now, Vice President Lyndon Johnson is on board Air force One being sworn in to serve as the thirty-sixth president of the United States.

Suddenly there's a rush of sound in my ears, like the roar of Bunna's plane crashing somewhere far off in the mountains, hard and final, echoing over and over.

They never found his body. They never did.

I have to get out of here, I think. *Right now.*

I have to get away from this fish that isn't our fish and these strangers' voices talking about a person we never knew, dying thousands of miles away, their voices as brittle as tin. I shove my chair from the table and leave, all alone.

And now I'm sitting on the edge of my bed, clutching my pillow, glad I'm alone because it feels like somebody just punched me in the gut. I really hate it when people try to talk to me when I'm hurting, especially white people, even the nice ones. Why do they always think it helps to talk to people when they're hurting?

I've got my feather pillow wadded up so tight, it'll probably shoot off like a bullet if I let go, and now I'm punching it, just for the heck of it, my hard fist punching that ball of broken feathers. It feels good. That's when I realize I'm not alone. Father Flanagan is standing in the door, watching me.

"Are you all right, Luke?"

"Yeah."

"You're not alone, you know. The whole country is feeling the same way you're feeling."

I nod, even though it's not true. The whole country has nothing to do with how I'm feeling. My feelings are not about President Kennedy, but I can't say this to Father, who's stooped forward like he's carrying the weight of Kennedy's death on his back.

"I'm okay," I say.

Father doesn't believe me. I can see it in his eyes. "It's a hard thing, Luke, but it's better not to isolate yourself. We all need to be together at a time like this." He straightens slowly, like it hurts.

I nod again, but I don't move. I just sit there holding that dumb pillow while Father stands halfway out the door, like he's not quite sure what to do next. All of sudden these words come shooting out of my mouth: "Father, can I call home?"

Father sighs with relief, I think. "Certainly, Luke. I'm sure we can arrange it. No one's in the office right now. You may use that phone."

Father's right. No one's in the office. Everyone else is huddled up together in the cafeteria, still listening to the static-filled news from Washington, D.C.

I dial the number, and suddenly I'm remembering how it was after Bunna died, right after his plane went down and they were still trying to figure out what happened and trying to get the news to the families. They let me call home that time, too. At first I didn't think I'd be able to talk, but it was so good to hear Mom's voice. I close my eyes now, warming myself on the memory.

Mom had been working at Smythe's Café, which is more like old man Smythe's home, because it's the only place in town that's got a phone, and a lot of people hang out there. When I called that time, some guy I didn't recognize had answered the phone and handed it to Mom without a word.

The line between Sacred Heart and the café was scratchy

with static that time, just like it is now with the radio. Mom's voice had sounded scared and confused.

"Amau?" she had said, using my old nickname.

She sounded like a person not quite awake, a person unsure about what's real life and what's dreaming.

"Amau?" Her voice had wavered. "That you?"

There was this lump in my throat the size of an iceberg, and I was suddenly so homesick, I could barely breathe.

"Yeah, Mom. It's me."

Suddenly, I had to pull the phone away from my ear because Mom was screaming so loud it hurt, screeching like a hundred thousand seagulls. Calling out for Uncle Joe and for every other uncle, aunt, and cousin I got like they were all right there, sitting in the café with her, waiting. And maybe they were.

"Joe, Mae, come here! It's Amau! Anna! Look who's on this phone right here! Dora! Dora! It's Amau! He's alive! Isabel! He's alive! He's alive, Rachel—come hear! Right now! Alice— guess who this is right here, it's Amau! He's still alive!"

I'd forgotten how many relatives I had until right at that exact minute when Mom started punctuating every other word with their names.

"Esther! Donald! It's Amau. Helen! Amau? Amau, is that really you?"

"Yes, Mom. It's me."

"Oh praise God, we thought you died. . . . Joe! Joe! Come here right now! *Qilamik!*"

The sound of her voice taking off across the phone line

like a fast car without a driver had made me start to laugh, crying at the same time. And in between the laughter and the tears, I was feeling every kind of feeling there was to feel, like I was fully alive for the first time since Bunna died. It felt really good and hurt really bad, both at the same time.

Suddenly I realize that the phone in my hand has quit ringing.

"Hello? HELLO?"

I had gotten so lost in remembering, I'd forgotten that I was calling again.

"Hello, I . . ." Suddenly, I don't know what to say or who to say it to. My thoughts and feelings are wadded up inside so tight that the words get squashed flat.

"Smythe's place. Hello?" It's Uncle Joe's voice, rich as whale meat.

"Uncle Joe?"

"Luke? That you? Hey, guy! When you coming home?"

"I'm not sure," I croak, almost ready to cry for happiness, it's so darned good to hear his voice. "Christmas maybe?"

"Yeah well, you have to come home," he says.

"I'm going to have to work hard next break to get enough money to get home," I say. But my voice catches on the word *home*. Then there's another silence. A silence that feels as long as forever.

Them damn Catholics.

I'm not sure if he really muttered it or not, but all of a sudden it feels like we turned a corner somehow.

"Hey, guess what?" Joe says suddenly. "Guess what I got now—a new kinda rodeo."

Rodeo?

"Yeah," Joe says, laughing suddenly at some joke of his own. "Rodeo with horses, mechanical horses, just like you guys got down there at that school."

I don't tell him that we don't got no rodeo at Sacred Heart School, mechanical or other. I just smile because something in his voice makes me feel like laughing. The sound of Uncle Joe, just being himself, is suddenly the best thing in the whole world. If he wants to think we got cowboys with our Indians here, let him.

"Rodeo just like the Indians got. Just like them cowboys. Eskimo rodeo." Then he laughs long and loud.

And Uncle Joe's laughter, smooth as seal oil, reaches all the way across the two mountain ranges that separate us, across all the rivers, right up into the office here at Sacred Heart School, where I stand in the growing darkness, smiling.

"No kidding," Joe says. "Eskimo rodeo. And you sure can catch caribou with this thing."

"Caribou?" I have no idea what he's talking about.

"Sure," Joe says. "Bring that old gun with you when you come home, and I'll show you how it works. Pretty slick."

Suddenly there's a lump in my throat as big as Sacred Heart School. Joe doesn't know about his gun, the gun that was supposed to be mine when I got old enough to take the kick.

I already took the kick.

"The gun was with Bunna, Joe," I whisper.

"What?" Joe says.

I can tell by the way his voice cracks that he heard me, but I say it again, anyhow. "It was in the plane. With Bunna."

And then there's another silence, like his voice got cut off. It's a silence empty as fog that reaches down across the God-forsaken tundra, over the mountains that claimed my brother and straight through this valley prickly with blue black spruce.

"Well, hey," says Joe, like he's warming his voice up. "Never mind that old gun. Just a piece of tin, right? Wait'll you see this new one I got."

I don't say anything.

"Luke?"

"Yeah?" It's all I can manage.

"Hey, this new gun?" Uncle Joe's voice sounds shaky. I nod as if he could see me. "You know what? It's got a sight that's never more than a hair from right. No jokes. Wait'll you try it."

It's totally dark now, but when I step out into the bitter-cold November night, it feels good, like coming home, somehow. The stars are pricking through the dark sky same as always, like nothing different has ever happened or ever will, and all of a sudden, I like that.

I have that letter, the one I saved. It's been there in the bottom of my drawer all this time—the letter from my little brother Isaac. In Texas. In Dallas, Texas. I never burned it like I said we should. I saved it. It wasn't much, but it's enough right now, enough to know that Isaac's alive somewhere, writing letters and swimming and climbing trees. Maybe even looking up at the same winter sky I'm looking at right now. Maybe even watching the same stars I'm watching—the ones in the hunter's constellation, bright as blazes. The one them *taniks* call Orion's Belt.

When they first told us how they named those three stars Orion's Belt, we used to wonder, me and Bunna. We knew those three were really hunters, and we wondered how those three hunters got trapped like that in a giant's belt.

I look up, and all of a sudden I'm laughing. Laughing and laughing all by myself, under the bright black sky. Them hunters are right there, and that giant Orion don't even know it. Them hunters aren't trapped at all. They're just waiting for the chance to take a shot. And when they do, that big old dumb Orion won't even stand a chance. Not one single chance.

I don't know how I know this, I just know.

I don't know how Isaac's gonna find his way home, all right, but he will. All of a sudden, I'm as sure about this as I am about anything. Isaac will find his way home. One way or another, we will all find our way home. Even Bunna.

Unchained Melody
MARCH 7, 1964

DONNA

The girl in the mirror is watching her hair fall to the floor in thick black ropes, falling to the scratchy snip-snip rhythm of Evelyn's scissors. The girl in the mirror concentrates hard on something off in the distance, as if she doesn't even hear the coiling and uncoiling sound of scissors cutting hair. She holds her chin up, aloof and certain.

Sixteen.

The girl in the mirror is and isn't Donna. She isn't the shy Donna, the timid Donna, the afraid-of-everything Donna. The girl in the mirror is a brave new Donna, a Donna people will have to pay attention to, a Donna who expects attention. The words she whispers inside have the force of volcanoes.

River. Rushing. Kiss. I'm re-creating myself with words, she thinks. *Words inside.*

Rose holds up a copy of *Life* magazine, that old one with the picture of Jackie Kennedy on the cover. She holds it up alongside the mirror, squinting at it hard, like she's trying to

make a positive identification, trying to identify that brand-
new girl.

"You look just like her, Donna," Rose says, slapping the
magazine down with decision.

Donna looks at Jackie Kennedy and tosses her hair. She
feels as sassy as a gull, so free she could spread her arms out
and drift upward without any effort at all. She imagines
herself looking down at that old magazine, which lies flat on
the floor, buried beneath a heap of long black hair. Her hair.

"What are you going to wear to the dance, Donna?"
Chickie asks.

Donna imagines herself naked, not needing clothes, warming herself like a mink in the spring sun.

"I don't really have anything," she says.

In fact, it doesn't matter one bit what the new Donna
wears, not one bit.

"You can borrow my pink sweater," Rose says.

"Perfect," Evelyn says, stepping back to eye the image
in the mirror like an artist trying to get perspective. Donna
smiles.

The new girl, the one in the mirror, smiles back. She is
ready.

In the cafeteria, Donna sits a little bit aside from the others,
listening to the clackety-clack of dinner trays and the tinkling
of silverware and the way it mingles with the soprano of girl
voices, chattering about the dance. She's wearing the soft pink
sweater that belongs to Rose and her own tight black skirt,

and she sits there on that hard cafeteria bench in that skirt and that sweater, feeling the curve of her spine as though it were the stem of some new kind of flower. She feels distant, not totally there, not totally anywhere.

Amiq's voice rises above the rest of the noises like a birdcall, sharp and distinct. Never mind what he's saying; the words don't matter. Donna is high up on a cliff somewhere, looking down into a billowing green valley, moving to the sound of Amiq's voice like a birch tree in the wind.

Waiting . . .

She has her eyes closed now. The gym is festooned with soft, dreamlike colors, and the music, which had been bright rock-and-roll a moment before, has transformed to match the colors—Donna can feel the change in the music with her whole body, like a change in the weather.

Warm spring rain.

It's "Unchained Melody," and the words wash over her, touching something deep inside, something fluttering and birdlike. Something so exquisite she hardly dares breathe for fear of dislodging it, of forcing it to fly.

Lonely rivers flow to the sea, to the sea. To the open arms of the sea . . .

Dancing with Amiq, Donna feels like she's finally come home. Like there's nothing else in the whole world except Amiq's body next to hers, Amiq's arm around her waist.

How did it come to be like this? She doesn't know, doesn't care. All that matters are Amiq's arms, holding her tight against the ebb and flow of the hungry music.

Lonely rivers sigh, wait for me, wait for me, I'll be coming home, wait for me . . .

She isn't sure what they've said, if anything, to bring them to this exact point, but before she even knows what's happening, she's following him out into the woods, wordlessly. She's never been this far out into the woods before, especially not at night, but Amiq knows the game trails blind, the way one meanders into another, disappearing and reappearing in strange ways, leading them deeper and deeper into the dark heart of the woods.

His feet are like fox feet or wolf feet, following the trails as if by instinct. As if by magic. Leading her in.

"Where are we going?" she asks at last, whispering, even though they're well beyond the range of parochial radar. Whispering as though they're in church, as though their hushed breathing is a new kind of prayer.

"Over there," Amiq says, nodding off into the darkness, as if darkness by itself is a destination.

When he pushes the spruce branches aside, there's a sudden rushing hole of light so bright, it takes her breath away—a spruce-lined room, lit by moonlight. They stand at its silvery center, transfixed.

"Close your eyes," he says, and Donna feels a little flash of fear—exciting fear. "It's okay," he says, and she knows right then that maybe it is okay or maybe it isn't, but it doesn't really matter. She closes her eyes, letting him guide her down onto the damp ground. The dark earth and rotting leaves smell of promise.

"Keep your eyes closed and lean back," Amiq says, and she lets him lean her back, her heart pounding, fighting the urge to pull away. His voice says *trust me* and more than anything else in the whole wide world she wants to trust Amiq.

She imagines a wild spring river, shattering the ice in the darkness that surrounds them.

"Now," he says. "Open them."

She opens her eyes and looks straight up into the impossibly star-filled sky. *"Oh!"*

The moon is huge. The moon is everything. The moon with Amiq eclipsing it, watching her with such dark intensity, she knows he's going to kiss her and he does—so softly it makes her feel like a flower opening in a warm rain.

When the kiss ends, she shivers involuntarily.

"You're cold," Amiq says, his voice protective. "Wait."

She watches the way he moves, stretching out his whole body, catlike, looking for something in the bank of spruce branches. Something he knows is there. Something hidden.

A half-empty bottle of vodka.

He takes a deep sip, offering it to her, and she tries it, too, even though it scares her worse than anything. The heat of it burns her throat, making her sputter, making her warm. He laughs softly.

She imagines that she'll always remember the way he traces his finger along the edge of her throat right then, tugging tenderly at the slender chain, pulling the medallion out from beneath her sweater, still warm from her breasts, holding it tight in the palm of his hand as though warming himself on it.

He studies it carefully, then looks directly at her. There's a question in his eyes. It's a question Donna wants to hear, a question she's afraid to hear. She looks at the little medal, lying in the palm of his hand, wishing she knew the right answer.

"Saint Christopher," she says, "the patron saint of travelers."

"I'm a traveler," he whispers. And then he drinks the rest of the vodka in one long gulp and leans over, kissing her. But this time the tenderness is gone, replaced by something else, something hard and demanding. Something darker than the river below, and burning like vodka.

Something that has nothing to do with her, nothing at all.

He isn't kissing *her* anymore—that's what she realizes all of a sudden. The vodka has gotten in the way and it isn't her at all. It's only his *idea* of her—slurred and generic—a quiet girl named Donna who's easy to look at. And his idea is all mixed up with her own idea of a brave new Donna, doing the kinds of things the old Donna never did. And both Donnas are mashed up together into something that has nothing to do with her. Nothing at all.

She pulls away from him.

"No, baby," he pleads. "No."

She stands up, brushing the pine needles off of Rose's pink sweater.

"We have to go back," she says.

But she doesn't go anywhere, because suddenly, there's a

sound.

"Amiq? You here?"

It's Luke, standing there in the clearing, looking at Donna and then at Amiq.

"They sent me to find you," Luke says.

The way he says it makes Amiq sit up slowly, like he doesn't want to but has no choice.

"What happened," he says.

"It's your dad," Luke says. "They called. He took off ten days ago. Traveling inland. Can't find him."

"Drinking," Amiq says, looking at Donna, dead sober now.

Luke shrugs. "Looks like it."

Amiq glares off into the dark woods.

"You know—," Luke starts.

"Shut up," Amiq snaps. "Just shut the hell up." He glares at Luke. Glares at the whole dark world. "He's probably sleeping it off in a cabin somewhere. My old man's tough as a wolverine."

Donna looks at the empty vodka bottle. Amiq looks at it, too.

Off in the distance somewhere, kids are still dancing. A door opens, and music drifts through the trees like smoke.

"Why do the birds go on singing . . . "

"My old man can survive anything," Amiq snaps.

Anything.

A Weak Spot or a Secret Strength
MARCH 12, 1964

LUKE

Luke is in the woods, lying on the sun-speckled ground, trying not to think heavy thoughts—trying not to feel the kinds of things heavy thoughts always make him feel—but it's impossible, because thinking and feeling are roped together now, roped together with something heavy. As soon as he starts to think, the hurt rises to the surface like a dead body, and as soon as he is reminded of the hurt, he can't help but think the kinds of thoughts that make it worse.

It goes round and round like that. Like a dog chasing its tail.

He'd been boxing that morning with Sonny, and that had helped. Father Mullen had been watching, the way he always watched, and they were boxing just like Father had taught them to. No mercy. Luke's body had been flexed hard as a fist, his mind focused, his feelings turned off. That's what Luke liked best about boxing. To box well, you had to turn your feelings off.

Now, lying on his back in the piney woods, he takes a deep breath and tries to make himself feel, again, the cold control of a boxer. Make his mind forget everything else, even that one thing that had happened after they finished boxing.

He was dancing back and forth, Sonny's movements like a shadow of his own, both of them waiting for the other to leave an opening. Both of them closed. Luke's fists coiled up so tight against his face they felt spring-loaded. Sonny swaying back and forth like a bear.

Luke could feel the punch, simmering deep inside, his feet shifting into place, his eyes locking onto Sonny's. Winding up. But just as his arm left his side, Sonny shoved a sudden jab. Luke hadn't even seen it coming. Sonny was just too fast.

Luke's return caught Sonny square in the nose, all right, but before he could finish it off, Sonny threw another punch. A perfect uppercut, shoving Luke right up off the floor and slapping him down like a fallen tree.

Sonny was left-handed, like a polar bear. In the heat of the match, Luke had forgotten and been caught off guard. Twice. He fell into Sonny hard, and they both went down and it was over, Sonny sitting on the floor, and Luke shoving himself upright, wiping blood from his nose. Both of them grinning and breathless.

It felt good. Like together they'd whipped something. Something important. Like they'd been working together, trying to move something huge, and it had suddenly broken loose and rolled away.

"Short match," Father said. Father Mullen did not like short matches.

"Sonny's got a mean left hook," Luke said, giving Sonny a sideways grin.

Sonny stood up, reached down, and grabbed Luke by the wrist, pulling him up, grabbing him hard. And that's when it happened.

Mullen was saying something, and Sonny was saying something else, and Luke understood that maybe he was supposed to be saying something back, but he couldn't because all of a sudden his ears were echoing and the sound of their voices was receding.

We lived in the dark that time, underground. We lived underground because it was too cold on the surface, too cold to even go outside, some days. The leader had to test the cold first, licking a spot on his wrist and sticking it up and out the door, past the thick layer of mastodon skins, sticking it out for just a second to see how fast the spot turned white with frostbite. Testing to see if it's too cold to search for meat that day. That's how we lived.

He saw it clearly.

Then he snapped back into the conversation, staring at Sonny and Father Mullen, who were still talking about boxing as if nothing unusual had happened.

I know this because I was there, Luke thought suddenly. *I was the leader, testing the safety of the frozen world with my own skin. I was there.*

"Your opponent will always have a weak spot," Father Mullen was saying. "Remember that."

Now, lying on his back in the woods, Luke thinks about this from all angles, his eyes still closed, his wrist stinging.

My wrist is a weak spot, Luke thinks. *Or maybe it's a strength, a secret strength.*

Or maybe it's both.

Our Story

"Look, Father."

Junior put the newspaper on Father Flanagan's desk. It was wrinkled, like dirty laundry, but the headline still rolled across it, sturdy as a tank: "Project Chariot Still On."

It was the front page of the first issue of *Tundra Times,* a newspaper covering Native news statewide. The editor was Junior's uncle. Junior had been saving it for just the right moment, the moment when he would have enough nerve to tell Father about the stories he wanted to write, now that they had started a school newspaper.

"That's very interesting, Junior," Father said.

Father obviously didn't know much about Project Chariot. Project Chariot was *interesting* the way a bear about to tear into somebody's gut is *a concern.*

"They were going to do a nuclear blast up north," Junior offered.

"Ummm?" said Father, erasing a mark in his grade book.

Junior's words did not carry the kind of force he wanted them to carry. They never did. Junior picked up the paper and shuffled to his desk in the back of the class, where he sat between Sonny and Amiq, an easy place for a person like Junior to disappear. He imagined a tape recorder rolling, the words he wanted to say, loud and clear and inescapable.

"They were going to blow it up," Amiq said.

Junior frowned.

"Blow up what?" Sonny said.

"Cape Thompson, right south of Point Hope," Amiq said.

"What?"

Amiq leaned over next to them like he was sharing a state secret. "Blow it right off the globe," he whispered. "With a bunch of A-bombs. Bigger than Hiroshima."

Luke turned around to look. Some of the other kids turned around, too, wide eyed.

Bombs?

"Right where we always hunt," Junior added, wishing he'd been the one to make them look.

"*Operation Plowshare,*" Amiq said, leaning back onto his chair with a smug smile. "That's what they call it."

Junior looked at Amiq, annoyed. How come Amiq always had to know everything about everything? And how come everybody always heard what Amiq said but barely even noticed when Junior said the same thing? And to make matters worse, Amiq was right, too. Project Chariot had been part of a government program called Operation Plowshare.

"You know, *plow*-share," Amiq said, emphasizing the

word. "They drop some bombs to plow out a harbor, nice and peaceful." His voice was neither nice nor peaceful.

"Plowshare?" Sonny said.

"It's in the Bible," Luke said quietly. "In Isaiah."

Amiq reached over and grabbed Junior's newspaper right off his desk without even asking. Junior frowned and adjusted his glasses.

"They said they were gonna use Operation Plowshare to demonstrate the peaceful use of nuclear weapons," Amiq hissed, grabbing Junior by the shoulders so violently that he nearly fell off his chair. "Right here." He stabbed at the paper with his finger, right where it said "Nuclear Blast" in large letters.

Junior wanted to punch him.

Amiq shoved the paper back onto Junior's desk and slapped Junior on the back. Father turned sideways, eyeing the two of them and noticing, for the first time, Junior's newspaper.

Amiq smiled smoothly and lifted it up for Father to see.

"The editor is Junior's uncle," he told Father. He nudged Junior.

"Can I do a story, Father?" Junior croaked. "For the school paper? About this one?" He looked down as he said it, his face growing warm, waiting for Father to dismiss the idea. Father probably wouldn't think a person like Junior could write about something as important as a nuclear blast.

"Yes, that would be good, Junior. A story about your uncle's newspaper," Father said.

Junior opened his mouth, then shut it again. A story about

the newspaper—that's not what he meant. But Father already had his back turned. Amiq leaned over and tapped the headline in Junior's uncle's paper: "Project Chariot Still On."

"You ought to do a story on *that*," Amiq said.

Luke sat in the library with Sonny, Michael O'Shay, and Amiq, staring at Amiq's collection of *Anchorage Times* news clippings, each one cut out neatly to the exact shape of its story. Amiq had laid them out like puzzle pieces.

"Eskimos in Game Law Revolt," cried one headline. "Officials Say Eskimos Warned on Duck Killing," another scolded. Luke's Uncle Joe was right up front in one of the pictures, smiling the same way he smiled when he told Luke that Catholics ate horse meat.

Duck killing. Luke remembered the three dozen ducks he and Uncle Joe had caught one spring. They had not called it duck killing.

Giving away all those ducks had been just like Christmas; they gave ducks to everyone. Some of the people they gave ducks to hadn't had any fresh meat all winter. When Luke thought about rich people, he always remembered handing out all those ducks, the smell of duck soup everywhere.

The *Anchorage Times* story said 138 Eskimo hunters had turned themselves in to the game warden in Barrow, waiting to be arrested for catching ducks out of season. They did it because they were protesting a law that made it illegal to hunt ducks in the spring and fall, the only times the ducks were in Alaska. One of the newspaper stories called it the Duck-In.

Luke studied the picture. The hunters were waiting in line in front of the game warden. The one at the head of the line was signing a piece of paper. Every single hunter held a dead duck. Uncle Joe was standing in the front of that picture, off to one side, holding his duck up high, like it was some kind of victory symbol. Grinning straight into the camera with a look that made Luke smile.

It made Amiq smile, too. "I like this guy," he said. "Fearless."

His dad would've liked the look on that guy's face, too, Amiq thought. *Like he's not afraid of anything. Like he could ask to get arrested and grin about it.*

Luke nodded. *That's how he is, all right.*

There was something about that picture that just forced you to notice it. Those hunters were all Luke's family, too—uncles and great uncles, his mom's cousins and Uncle Joe's buddies—and Uncle Joe seemed so alive, bigger than life. Like he could just step right out of the newspaper and march into the room with all those hunters behind him.

Fearless.

Luke looked up and blinked with a sudden realization. *When they were all together like that, what was there to be afraid of?*

"They got a jail in Barrow big enough for that many hunters?" Michael O'Shay asked, leaning over Luke's shoulder.

"Not a chance," Amiq said. They would of had to take 'em to Fairbanks."

"They'd have to pay for one heck of a big plane to send

all those guys to Fairbanks," O'Shay said, and suddenly Amiq started laughing. Laughing and laughing the way Luke's uncle must have laughed. Laughing for both him and his dad.

"All them hunters and their ducks!" he cried. "Don't forget the ducks!"

"You don't need permission," Amiq was saying.

They were sitting in the *Sacred Heart Guardian* editorial office, which was actually Father Flanagan's classroom. Chickie and Sonny were *Sacred Heart Guardian* reporters, and Junior was the editor. Amiq wasn't anything.

Junior looked at Amiq but didn't say a word. Who'd said anything about permission?

"Father said I should write about my uncle's newspaper," Junior said.

"Yeah, but that's not the *real* story," Amiq said.

Junior bristled. The real story? Junior could feel the real story. He could almost hear it, in fact. It whispered in the back of his mind, like a tape machine rolling with the sound turned down low. He could hear the clacking sound of tape on the reel, but he couldn't hear the words, because Amiq was talking too much.

Junior turned away, tuning Amiq out, thinking about the Duck-In. One of the papers had called it "a civil disobedience action," which was a curious phrase. How could people be civil and disobedient at the same time?

Junior thought about the hunters. First one hunter had been arrested for catching a duck out of season, and then the rest got upset, and they all showed up, holding ducks. They weren't trying to break the law, like the Anchorage papers said. They were just sticking together, following their own law.

That was the real story, Junior thought. *Or was it?*

And what was the real story behind Project Chariot—the story *he* wanted to tell? Junior wasn't exactly sure. But he was sure about one thing: he could find the real story just fine without any help from Amiq.

"The story Father told me to write is the story about the new newspaper," Junior said again. He said it just to shut Amiq up. He needed time to think.

"Is that how your uncle got a new newspaper, by writing the stories somebody told him to write?" Amiq said.

Junior adjusted his glasses. "I guess," he said.

Amiq grinned and shook his head, like he knew better. "You write it down and I'll help keep you honest," he said.

Chickie looked at Junior and rolled her eyes.

"I can write my own story," Junior said.

But his jaw was set so hard, it felt like he was going to have to grind the words out sideways.

When Father Flanagan read Junior's story, all he did was frown and scratch his head.

"This isn't quite what I was expecting, Junior."

Junior swallowed hard and nodded. Amiq, in the corner of the room, grinned.

"This isn't the kind of story we run in the *Sacred Heart Guardian.* And it's not very uplifting, either, is it?" Father said.

"A bunch of grown men, breaking the law—who wants to hear about that?"

Junior nodded again, his chest tightening.

"The *Guardian* is for our students, Junior. Our students are interested in hearing about your uncle's newspaper because he's your uncle. This other stuff"—Father waved his arm like he was shooing off mosquitoes—"this other stuff belongs in your uncle's paper, not in ours."

Junior looked down and nodded a third time, biting his cheeks to keep the tears away. He could feel Amiq, over there in the corner, watching. They were all watching. He lifted his chin and adjusted his glasses.

"Write one about the paper, will you, Junior?" Father said.

Junior nodded and swallowed. The lump in this throat was sharp as ice.

"What about you, Chickie? What are you writing about?" Father asked.

"I'm writing about the new desks Sister Mary Kate got, the ones that school in Anchorage donated." She said it fast, watching Junior out of the corner of her eye as if writing about new desks made her feel guilty all of a sudden.

"Great idea," Father said, shuffling through a pile of papers on his desk. "What's the headline?"

Chickie looked at Junior. Junior, after all, was the editor.

"Providence Strikes Again," Amiq said loudly. "That's the headline."

Chickie glared at Amiq, and Amiq winked.

"Clever," Father said without looking up. "Very catchy. Sister Mary Kate and her acts of Providence . . . now *there's* an uplifting story."

Father scooped up his papers and slid out of the room. "You kids keep at it," he called back.

Amiq was hovering behind Chickie like a big crow, reading her story.

"Sister Mary Kate and her student volunteers are up to their elbows in sandpaper and varnish, and from out of the dust, shiny new desks are arising," Amiq read.

Chickie frowned and swatted him away, but you could tell she was proud of her story. It *was* good.

"Sounds like all that dust is gonna get stuck to the varnish on their elbows," Amiq said.

Junior grinned at the image, resisting a sudden urge to laugh out loud.

"Is not," Chickie squeaked, pulling at the sleeve of her sweater and swatting, again, at Amiq. She reminded Junior of an indignant little squirrel.

"And those desks look just like new, too," Chickie chittered.

Amiq smiled innocently. "Absolutely."

Junior ducked his head, biting his cheeks to keep from laughing.

Amiq began pacing around the room like he was being propelled by some kind of creative energy, circling over Junior like a bird of prey. Swooping down so suddenly it made

Junior flinch. Then he landed on the chair next to Junior's and watched him impatiently, like he expected Junior to do something. Something *he* wanted done.

Junior bent his head over his paper and began scribbling furiously. He wasn't really writing anything important; he was just trying to distract Amiq, trying to *hear* the words to his story. They still seemed to be rolling along in the back of his mind, just out of earshot. If Amiq would just leave him alone, maybe he could hear them. But Amiq refused to be distracted. Every time Junior ducked his head lower, Amiq ducked his head, too, sticking his nose right up next to Junior's paper until pretty soon it seemed like Junior was either going to have to stop writing or start writing on Amiq's nose.

Junior put his pen down and looked at Amiq.

"It was a good story, the one you wrote," Amiq said.

Junior shook his head. No, it wasn't a good story. It hadn't said what Junior had wanted it to say. Junior realized this with sudden clarity.

"You aren't going to let them bully you around, are you, Junior?" Amiq said.

Junior sat up straight, adjusted his glasses, and looked Amiq right square in the eye. "No one's bullying me around," he said.

"You remember that story about the duck hunters?" Amiq said.

Junior nodded.

"Civil disobedience, just like you said."

"I never said that," Junior pointed out.

"And it only works when writers do their job and write about it," Amiq said.

Junior blinked with surprise. He was a writer! No one had ever called him that before. He liked the sound of it. He liked it a lot.

"Those Barrow hunters weren't trying to be disobedient," Junior said. It felt like he was speaking with a brand-new authority, the authority of a *writer.* "They were just trying to feed their family."

He started to correct himself—he'd meant to say *families*—but then he started thinking about the word *family.* Family started out in one village and spread to another and then another. Spread throughout the whole state of Alaska and even down into the Lower 48, some families. And they were all related, too. Just like Luke's uncle having a cousin in Barrow that time they did the Duck-In.

The human family—he'd heard that phrase before, too. Suddenly the idea of people just trying to feed their family took on new meaning. He thought about Project Chariot— the force of the blasts shooting out into the ocean, where people catch whales to feed all the families. And he thought about the ice cellars where they stored whale meat and *maktak* for the whole community family, and about the bomb shelters where people were going to hide from the bomb that threatened everybody—the whole human family.

He saw the mushroom cloud of a bomb, like he'd seen it in *Life* magazine, and the feathery spray of the whale . . .

Amiq was still talking, all right, but Junior barely even heard him. Junior was recording sentences in his mind. They were the kind of sentences no one could ever ignore. He picked up the neatly typed story Father Flanagan had dismissed and tossed it into the trash. Amiq watched him with a look—a look of what? Surprise? Shock? No, Junior decided; the word was *astonish*. Amiq looked astonished.

"You can't just throw it away!" Amiq's voice rose. "Just because Father said so?"

"Yes, I can." Junior said.

"Stand up for yourself for once," Amiq said.

But Junior wasn't listening. Junior had started to tell another story in his mind. It was like talking into the tape recorder, but this time, a tape recorder with the sound *on*. The reel went round and round, and people were listening. He couldn't see them, but he could feel them. They were out there, somehow, listening to his words. At first it was just the people in his village—his *aaka* and all his aunties and uncles—people who knew him and understood the story. But then there were others—strangers from Fairbanks and Anchorage, maybe even Seattle—a whole audience of people who thought the way Father thought. He could feel them leaning forward, as if they were trying to understand. And it was up to him to tell this story in a way they *could* understand, because he was the storyteller. He was the writer.

"You could send it to the *Tundra Times*," Amiq said.

"Wrong audience," Junior said. Everyone looked at Junior, and their faces all said the same thing: *Audience?*

Junior took a deep breath and looked down. But the tape kept rolling.

The headline for Junior's story read "From the Ice Cellar to the Bomb Shelter."

When Father Flanagan read it, he smiled nervously.

It started with the image of Junior's *aaka* eating fresh duck soup, meat the young hunters brought her because that's what hunters do, they feed the people, especially the old ones. And it ended with a nuclear blast bright enough to blind them all. And there was a lot of stuff in between, too, both sad and happy.

When Chickie read it, it made her think of Bunna. She wasn't sure why, it just did. When Luke read it, he was glad Junior had said something about iodine-131 and the way those guys had put wires on them. He just hoped people would hear what Junior was saying and *do* something. He wasn't sure what he wanted them to do. But when he read it a second time, he realized that in fact Junior had never said a single word about iodine-131.

How had Junior done that, he wondered—said something without actually saying it?

"Excellent writing, Junior," Father said. "Very good, actually." He looked up and frowned off into the distance. "But you know when you write for a newspaper, you are supposed to convey facts, not express opinions."

Junior looked up. Father's face was smiling, and his blue eyes were kindly, but Junior felt like he'd just been exposed in front of everyone. He looked down at his story, suddenly embarrassed. He had expressed his opinion, and newspaper stories aren't supposed to have opinions. It was like getting caught with your fly down. He looked away.

"This business about the whales and everything," Father said, waving his hands. "That Chariot project was not about bomb shelters and whales, it was about economic development for the State of Alaska—making a new harbor with atomic energy—and look, you haven't mentioned that *anywhere* in this story."

Junior blinked in surprise. For a minute he wasn't even sure that Father was talking about the story he, Junior, had written. It felt like Father was talking about something else altogether. Father had his own opinion, all right, and it was very different than Junior's. The more Junior thought about it, the more hopeless it seemed. Nothing but opinions, people's opinions—some right and some wrong, depending on how you looked at it.

"Are we going to put Junior's story in the *Guardian*? Chickie asked.

"Well . . . ," Father said. His voice turned up at the end in a way that made the answer clear even though he hadn't said it.

Junior's story suddenly looked worthless to him. What was the point, anyhow? Project Chariot was still on, duck hunting was still illegal, and people like Amiq's dad still disappeared. And other people even died, like Bunna. What difference did words make? Junior shoved the story back into his notebook and stood up. It was time for lunch, and Junior suddenly felt a deep, nameless hunger.

"Let me see it," Amiq said. "Let me see your story." They were walking down the hall toward the cafeteria, and Junior was still clutching his notebook. He pulled the story out and handed it to Amiq. Why not? Who cared, anyhow?

Amiq's dad was still missing. They had looked and looked, and they hadn't found him anywhere, not even a clue, and now they had quit looking. Amiq looked out the classroom window, frowning. Junior's story had made a lot of sense, but the world itself made no sense at all.

Watching Luke fidgeting at his desk, Amiq thought about Bunna, about the first time he'd seen the two of them. They'd been sitting side by side on the plane. No—that wasn't right. Luke had been sitting on one side and Bunna had been sitting on the other. Their little brother sat in the middle. What was that kid's name, anyhow? Amiq couldn't remember.

He glanced at Luke, who sat there rubbing his wrist and looking bored.

"What was your little brother's name—the other one?" Amiq asked him.

Luke looked up, surprised. "Isaac," he said.

Amiq tried out the name. He liked the way it started breathless in the back of his throat, then clicked sharp against the roof of his mouth. "Isaac. Yeah."

He wrote it on a piece of paper. ISAAC. And then he wrote

some more. At first it was more like doodling, but the more he wrote, the more he thought about brothers and fathers missing and missing people in general, people who should have been part of the family but were gone. People who just burned up or got lost or died, one way or another.

Before he knew what he'd done, he'd written something that looked like a plea. No, it looked more like an ad—a missing persons ad. It only had one name on it—Isaac—but he'd written it for all the people they were missing, somehow.

Amiq was surprised by what he'd written—he wasn't the writer. And true enough, his writing wasn't very long and it wasn't at all fancy, but it was right. Just right.

He centered it on his desk for everyone to see and stood up feeling light as a bird.

Let them just see it. Let them all see it.

Luke watched Amiq leave the room in the thick press of students. He stood up, leaned over Amiq's desk, and looked at the words scrawled across the top of the page lying there.

Isaac

What made Amiq remember Isaac all of sudden? Then he read what Amiq had written and blinked, surprised. It felt like a huge weight had suddenly been lifted from his chest. He'd lived with it for so long that until it flicked its heavy tail and disappeared, he'd forgotten it was there.

He picked up Amiq's paper, breathed deeply, and tucked it into his book. These words didn't belong on Amiq's desk.

They belonged with the story Junior had written. They needed Junior's story for backup. No, *backup* wasn't quite right. The audience that was going to read Amiq's story needed to read Junior's story first. That's how it worked. The story Junior said didn't belong anywhere belonged with Amiq's.

That's what Luke decided, walking down the hall toward the library.

Father Mullen was mad. Who was responsible for *this*. He waved a newspaper at them. It was the "Letters to the Editor" section of the *Dallas Morning News*, a newspaper none of them had ever even seen before. The headline read: "From the Ice Cellar to the Bomb Shelter: Seeking Missing People." It was signed "Aamaugak, a student at Sacred Heart School in Alaska."

Who was Aamaugak?

Looking at the headline, Junior felt all the blood drain from his face. For a couple of long seconds, he couldn't even breathe. Maybe he would suffocate. Or throw up. He looked at Amiq. Amiq looked at him and shrugged, smiling the way he always smiled. Like everything was all part of some grand plan he'd always had.

"I'm sure there's some explanation," Father Flanagan was saying, standing next to Father Mullen, ringing his hands. Junior could tell that Father Flanagan was trying hard not to look at him.

"We will sit here until we get the *truth*," Father Mullen said.

They all sat, rigid in their seats, trying not to eye each other. The silence roared in their ears like a military plane. A plane full of weapons landing. Father Mullen's gaze swept across the room, pausing on Amiq's downturned head. Amiq sat still. Calm and certain. Then, very slowly and very deliberately, he stood up.

Luke looked at him and frowned, shaking his head with a movement so slight, most people wouldn't have noticed it. Amiq looked away.

"I'm responsible," Amiq said in a loud voice. "I did it."

Junior let out a big sigh of relief. He hadn't realized that he'd been sitting there with his fists clenched, holding his breath. He was suddenly grateful that he was the kind of kid people never seemed to notice.

But with his fists unclenched, he felt strangely flat and deflated. And then, just as suddenly, he was mad. Amiq had done it again! Even though he'd been trying to protect Junior, he'd done it again. Made Junior invisible. Made Junior's writing invisible.

Junior raised his hand. It seemed at first that no one even noticed him, way in the back, his skinny arm poised like a question mark.

Father Mullen looked at him with curiosity. "Junior?"

"Actually, sir," Junior said, shoving at his glasses. He saw Donna's face, closed as a book, and looked at Leo Pete, scared as a rabbit, and at Amiq, who frowned at him and said *no* with his eyes.

Yes?" Father said.

"I wrote it," Junior said. The words seemed to fly out of his mouth. He looked straight at Father, thinking about his story, which was now a newspaper story no matter what anyone said. The tape was rolling in his head again, and he could hear it loud and clear: the word *family.* Suddenly his story seemed to belong to everyone, even Amiq. "In a way, sir . . . in a way, we all wrote it."

He hadn't meant to say that last part out loud.

Leo Pete shuffled awkwardly, and the girls looked at Junior with betrayed eyes, then they looked at Father with looks that said, *"We never!"* Amiq grinned at Luke.

Luke stared back. "It's true," he said.

Father Mullen looked at Junior and smiled. "That's very noble of you, son," he said. Then he told Amiq to follow him.

Civil Disobedience
SPRING 1964

Amiq was piling stuff together on his bed, acting like he was all alone in the room—all alone in the world, maybe. Acting like Luke and Sonny and the Pete boys didn't even exist. He was staring at the bed as he worked with a look that said he didn't see or hear any of them.

"What did you have to do that for?" Sonny said, finally. It wasn't a question; it was an accusation. Amiq flashed a look at Sonny.

"Because," Amiq said. His jaw snapped shut on the word with a force that made Leo Pete think of his uncle's steel traps.

"Pe-cuz," Sonny mimicked.

Amiq scowled. For a second it looked like he was going to punch Sonny. Then his eyes got dark and his face went hard, and you got the feeling they could do just about anything and it wouldn't touch him. Wouldn't even register.

Amiq's duffle sat gape-mouthed on the floor, and he started to cram it full of stuff: wrinkled clothes, broken pencils, a hunting knife and, unaccountably, a beat-up old copy of *The History of Alaska* left over from Father Flanagan's seventh-grade history class. He looked briefly at the book and grinned. It was not an amiable grin.

"President Seward paid the Russians $7,200,000 for something they didn't even own. A royal rip-off," he said, shoving the book underneath a wad of underwear. "Seward's Folly."

The Pete boys eyed each other uncomfortably.

"Folly?" Leo said.

"Means 'I jokes,'" Amiq said, no humor whatsoever in his voice. He eyed Sonny sidewise. "Least we never let them set foot on *our* land. Our grandfathers killed trespassers. *All of them.*"

Sonny leaned forward, tense. It wasn't entirely clear exactly who Amiq was including in the word *all.* But Amiq had already turned away from them like he never said it, punching dirty socks into the edges of his duffle.

"Somebody oughta beat the crap out of that guy," Sonny muttered, looking at the Pete boys as if daring one of them to do it.

"Don't bother," Amiq said, his back to Sonny. "I'm already gone."

His voice was flat, like he didn't even care. Which didn't sound at all like Amiq. *Not at all,* Luke thought. Watching his face, Luke felt a sudden feeling of helplessness reaching its icy fingers deep into his chest. No matter how he looked at it, he couldn't figure it out: Amiq had been willing to take all the responsibility—he had *wanted* to take it. But why? He'd written the missing-person ad, all right—the ad that said Isaac had been kidnapped—but Isaac was Luke's responsibility, and the story itself was Junior's. And the newspaper—well, that had nothing at all to do with Amiq. Luke had sent those stories in to the Dallas newspaper. So why did Amiq want to take the whole rap himself?

Father Mullen had said that people like Amiq didn't belong at Sacred Heart, and right now, watching the way Amiq stood there, his back to the world, zipping up his duffle, ready to run off into the dark of the night for who knows what, Luke thought maybe Father was right. Amiq was a lone ranger, and lone rangers belonged alone.

But what would happen to Amiq if he left them? Luke didn't know. All he knew for sure was that if Amiq were to leave right now, leave before they even had a chance to get him on a plane, he wouldn't go home. Not with his dad gone. If Amiq left now, he wouldn't even survive. Luke wasn't sure how he knew this, but suddenly he knew it as sure as he knew anything. He thought about Amiq's old man and Amiq's vodka and all the drunks on Two Street like the one they found passed out behind a bar one time, frozen solid.

If Amiq leaves here right now, that's exactly what's gonna happen to him. If Amiq leaves alone, it would be like sending him off to disappear—or die.

Maybe Sonny was right. Maybe Amiq needed somebody to beat some sense into him once and for all.

But when he looked from Amiq to Sonny, all he saw was a hard black web of anger, binding them both together in a stranglehold.

It made him think of Bunna, watching out the window of Sacred Heat's beat-up old bus that time. How mad he'd felt, watching Bunna roll away, his fists balled up against his side. *Mad and helpless.*

"Only dogs get mad," he muttered. He hadn't meant to say it, hadn't even thought it; it just came out. It's what his *aaka* used to say.

Then he thought of his little brother Isaac, riding off into the dark of another night, his nose pressed up against the window of a car. How scared he'd been, that time, standing there in the dark, watching. *Scared and helpless.* Knowing it would be forever. Just like with Bunna.

What good did it do to know things if nobody listened? What good did it do to know things when you weren't even sure what it was you knew or what to do about it?

That hard spot in his gut tightened. He imagined it like a lump of helpless fear and anger, frozen solid. Frostbite.

I'm the one who tests the weather, Luke thought suddenly. *They have to listen.*

He looked right at Amiq as hard as he could look. Without any anger, without any fear. Just knowing what he knew.

But Amiq wouldn't look at him.

"You don't have to do it," Luke said. "Not by yourself. That's how people die—going out alone." He thought of Amiq's dad.

"I know," Amiq said quietly.

"If you go out there now, all alone, it'll kill you."

Amiq looked up, finally. His face grew pale and helpless

for just a second. Then with a flick of anger, he threw his duffle over his shoulder and stalked out of the room. His whole body said it: *who cares?*

Luke thought of the ice age and how they'd survived it. He imagined a white circle of frostbite on his own wrist, like a warning sign or a badge. Something you could wave in someone's face: *See? Not safe. I'm the law.*

But when he looked at his wrist, he saw nothing.

It was late when Father Flanagan stuck his head into the room to tell them lights out. Later than usual. Nobody said a thing about the fact that Amiq wasn't there. They didn't have to. Father looked right at Amiq's empty bed and nodded.

"Go to sleep," Father said quietly. "The Lord will take care of him."

Father sounded so certain, it was hard not to believe him.

But we're supposed to take care of him, Luke thought. *Amiq is family.*

The thought was so loud, it startled him. He looked right at Sonny, and Sonny looked right back like maybe *he'd* heard the thought, too.

Father closed the door softly, and Luke leaned toward Sonny's bed. "Hey, man, he's our brother."

Sonny didn't answer, but he didn't go to sleep, either. The two of them just lay there, in the dark of night, watching shadows move while the others drifted off to sleep.

At last, Sonny sat up in the dark and spat out two words: *"Aw, hell."*

Luke could hear Sonny fumbling around in the dark for his shoes, muttering, "Stupid Eskimo. Stupid doggone Eskimo." But there wasn't any anger in his voice. Not a drop.

And Luke didn't feel helpless anymore, either.

"What time is it?" Junior murmured.

"It's the *right* time," Luke said, smiling to himself.

And Junior smiled, too, half awake and half asleep, squinting owlishly into the dark. "It is, isn't it?" he said.

The woods were dark, all right, but Sonny knew the way. Amiq, in fact, had been the one to show it to him. This thought made Sonny smile into the darkness. Made him laugh, almost. That crazy Eskimo and his Eskimo hideout. Hiding out from the Indians.

Well, not this Indian. Not this time.

He walked through the woods without a sound—not one single twig cracking, not one stone rolling.

Amiq was right where he knew he'd be, too. He hadn't even heard Sonny coming. Even now, he had no idea that Sonny was standing right behind him. He just sat there in his darkened hideout, staring morosely at the ground. Sonny leaned forward. Amiq wasn't just staring at the ground. He was holding something, something small that dangled from a slender chain and twinkled in the moonlight, and he was staring at an empty vodka bottle that lay on the ground by his feet. Looking at it hard, like he expected it to say something. That bottle had been there longer than Amiq had been staring at it, you could tell. Something about that pathetic old bottle and the way Amiq was hunched over it, clutching whatever it was he clutched, was just too funny. Sonny couldn't help it; he burst out laughing.

Amiq leaped up, the little chain swinging from his fingers like some kind of spent weapon.

"What the hell!" He glared at Sonny. "What are *you* doing here?"

Sonny grinned. "Looking for trespassers," he said.

Amiq stood there for just a second, his fists up at his chest like a boxer. Then he started laughing, laughing so hard he almost cried.

"Oughta beat the crap out of you," Amiq said, almost choking on the words.

"Try it," Sonny said.

"I jokes," Amiq said.

He looked down at his hand. It was Donna's necklace, Sonny realized, the one she always wore.

"Saint Christopher," Amiq said with a silly little grin. "The patron saint of travelers." And they both laughed. "Don't know how she managed to get it into my duffle. Or when."

Then the two of them just sat there in the dark woods, their backs to the empty bottle, staring at the river and at the necklace, swinging from the ends of Amiq's fingers like a bell.

"What kind of mess you got us in now, Amundson?"

"Ain't your mess, that's for sure."

There was a crack of branches, and suddenly Junior was there with them, with Luke right behind him.

"Yes it is. It's everybody's mess," Junior said.

He walked over to them in that tentative way he had and sat down right next to them, shoving his glasses up onto the bridge of his nose, like he was trying to apologize for something. With Junior, everything felt like an apology.

"We sort of had this idea," he said, taking his glasses off and cleaning them on his T-shirt. He gave Amiq a small, near-sighted smile. "Civil disobedience, just like you said."

And Luke, leaning up against a tree, smiled.

Old man Johnson, owner of Johnson's Lodge and Bait, gives Junior a funny look when he says he has some papers that need notarizing. For a long moment, Johnson doesn't say a word, just squints at the papers. Then he looks at Junior. Hard.

"Now, Junior," he says. "You don't expect me to believe that you had anything to do with that whole mess, do you? I sure never heard you talk like *this* before, the way this letter's written." He scowls at Amiq, standing there next to him, then looks back at Junior. "And that ad doesn't sound at all like you, either, Junior."

Mr. Johnson stands behind the counter of his store, which is attached to his lodge at the far end of the coffee shop. The sign that reads NOTARY PUBLIC hangs behind him on the log wall, framed. He doesn't even notice Luke, hunched up in the shadows in the corner of the room.

"You're not trying to say *you're* the one who wrote 'em both, are you?" Johnson says.

"Yes, sir," Junior says. "I am."

"Says here on this affidavit you're taking full responsibility for the whole thing. . . ."

"Yes, sir."

"Son, I don't think you want to do that."

Chickie picks this exact moment to stick her little blond head into the lodge and stroll breezily over to the counter, where she slides onto the stool right next to Junior as easy as if it's a classroom and the bell has just rung. She knows Mr. Johnson—he's an old friend of her dad's from back when they both worked for the same trading company.

"Oh, yes, Mr. Johnson, he does want to do that," she says sweetly. "And so do I."

"What!" Old man Johnson just about launches himself over the counter. "Are you saying the two of you wrote it together? Come on now, Chickie, you're daddy ain't gonna go for that at all, and you know it."

Chickie smiles. "Well, I'm afraid that just can't be helped," she purrs. "And anyhow, Swede ought to be used to me by now, don't you think?"

Johnson grins, despite himself, then frowns and shakes his head. "And you want me to notarize them?"

Junior can tell by the sound of his voice that Mr. Johnson is starting to feel trapped.

"Says right there you're a Notary Public," Chickie announces, waving her arm at the framed certification. "And I don't see why we should have to go all the way to town when you're right here." She looks up and smiles sweetly, like a little girl talking to her daddy.

Old man Johnson shakes his head, muttering, but it isn't an angry sound. Then he goes over to a shelf and pulls out his notary stamp.

"All right," he says. "Sit down. Let's get this over with. You just remember, now, that this here is a legal document, and you two will have to live with the consequences of it."

When Johnson says the word *consequences*, he turns to look at Amiq, but Amiq is no longer there. Amiq is outside helping Sonny round up the others—Rose and Evelyn, the Pete brothers and the rest—all of them waiting to sign affidavits.

Just like those duck hunters.

We are hunters, too, Amiq thinks, looking at them all and smiling: *hunters for justice.*

It feels, in fact, like one big communal hunting trip, with Junior as the unlikely guide, and the rest of them watching the horizon and waiting for their turn to shoot.

When Donna slips past him, Amiq tries to catch her eye, but she refuses to look. Even in the dark, though, he sees her blush. He doesn't think he's ever seen her blush before. He smiles to himself. Then he realizes that he's blushing, too.

Luke isn't outside with the others. He's right there, leaning up against the darkened wall inside, invisible almost, watching. As Amiq slips out the door, Luke steps forward, right up to the counter with the sign that offers LIVE BAIT and the cartoons about "the one that got away." He stares at one of the cartoons, old and yellowed, and picks up the pen.

"I'll be first," he says.

"Not sure why you want to get mixed up in this one, Luke," Johnson says.

"Yes, sir," Luke says, not really hearing Mr. Johnson and not hearing the sound of Amiq and Sonny and all the other kids just outside the door. Not hearing anything except the sound of a small silence deep inside.

He looks at the form, looks at that word *affidavit* and remembers, suddenly, that other affidavit, a long time ago, the one that followed Isaac. But it wasn't an affidavit, Sister had said—it was a permission form. Luke looks at the affidavit laid out on the counter and thinks about the word *permission*. How do you say *permission* in Iñupiaq, he wonders? If there is a word, he can't remember it, doesn't need it. He lifts the pen and leans forward. LEGAL NAME, the form asks.

Legal name? He puts the pen right there on that line and signs his name, his real Iñupiaq name, the one he left behind: *Aamaugak.* He hears the sound of it as the pen scratches the paper, the sound of his mother's voice, a warm, guttural buzz in the dusty darkness of Johnson's Lodge and Bait.

Sometimes there's nobody going to give you permission. Sometimes you just have to take it for yourself.

Johnson looks at his signature and frowns, but he doesn't say a word. Then he signs it himself and stamps it "notarized."

Aamaugak. Luke thinks. *What's so hard about that?*

As if on cue, everyone is now lined up behind him, waiting to sign. Everyone except Michael O'Shay, who is still sitting on the bench outside the lodge, staring off into the woods morosely until, finally, he's the only one left. Sonny sticks his head out the door and smiles at him broadly.

"Okay, O'Shay. Your turn, my man."

O'Shay frowns. "I don't think so. My dad would kill me."

"Come on, O'Shay, don't be so damn white."

O'Shay bristles. "As a matter of fact, I am white, and if I get expelled, I'll be dead and white."

"How the heck they gonna expel the entire student body?"

O'Shay looks off into the woods thoughtfully. Then he stands up.

"Oh, what the hell."

"Here's the real story, sir," Junior tells Father Mullen, handing him the stack of affidavits. "And we all wrote it."

And that was the truth, the whole truth. It was no longer just one person's opinion. It belonged to all of them.

Father leafed through the affidavits, and all he said was, "I see."

What else could he say?

"I see."

Good Friday

MARCH 27, 1964

Father Mullen needs a break. Lord knows he needs a break. He needs a break from all those brats and their nonsense. That's why he's here, isn't it, walking the deserted beach of Seward, Alaska, which seems suddenly calm. Too calm. He sighs, thinking unaccountably of his mother. He doesn't remember her, of course. He was just a baby. But sometimes, at odd moments, he feels her presence. It seems by turns to be both an admonishment and a comfort.

Lord knows he could use some comfort now.

He picks up a stone and tries to send it skating across the rolling, smooth skin of the sea the way he used to do on the pond back home in Missouri when he was a boy. It sinks on the first skip. He watches it, absently, thinking about those Native boys, the ones he's supposed to mold into Christians, the ones trying to break their thick, senseless skulls against the mold. The beach is full of flat, smooth stones perfect for skipping, but Father seems to have lost the knack.

In the sanctuary at Sacred Heart School, hundreds of miles

north of Seward, Father Flanagan pauses, briefly, to wonder if they aren't overdoing it a bit, making these kids sit
through Mass more than once in the same day. Even if it
is Good Friday. Making them say Mass every day, for that
matter. There are better ways to model Christian charity, one
would hope.

Luke Aaluk, in the bathroom at the Sacred Heart dorm,
doesn't think much of Christian charity, but he would agree
with the part about overdoing it. He stares at his reflection in
the steamy mirror of the shower room, altogether sick of stepping out of squeaky showers, freezing cold, of getting dressed
in stiff white shirts and choking ties and mumbling the words
to Mass over and over until none of it makes any sense in any
language. When he goes home, he'll for sure go the rest of his
life without ever taking one more single stinking shower or
wearing one more stiff white shirt or sitting through one more
mumbling Mass. That's his particular vow for this particular
Good Friday, and he thinks it's a good one.

Chickie Snow is not inclined to make vows right now. She
takes her cookie and her glass of milk and sits down neatly
at the table, all alone in the cafeteria. It's a secret she and
Sister Mary Kate share: her own private treat ever since that
time when she first came to Sacred Heart and got lost in the
woods.

Fresh cookies and milk.

Even though she hasn't said it out loud, she thinks of

Bunna and feels those words catch in her throat: *fresh cookies and milk.*

Milk. Bunna never liked milk.

Donna kneels on the cold floor of the Sacred Heart chapel, feeling that wordless sense of understanding that comes sometimes. She can't quite say what it is she understands, but it makes her feel happy, filled with a sense of belonging as wide as the ocean. It comes to her when she least expects it: in the hush of Sister Sarah's garden, in the sweet soprano of all their voices singing together, and right here, in the dusky, cold sanctuary with the swish of Father Flanagan's robes, whispering against the edge of it like slow waves on an endless beach.

Sister Sarah kneels, too, nearly invisible in the darkness. Her old joints ache, stiff against the chill air. When she kneels too long, it always hurts to stand again. On days like today, she wants to pray to put a stop to it all.

No, don't make me stand again. Let me go home.

Amiq, stepping out of the shower, studies his face in the mirror. The Saint Christopher medal Donna gave him hangs on the metal shelf below the mirror. *Saint Christopher Protect Us,* it pleads. Amiq only takes it off when he showers and hardly ever looks at it anymore. Like it's a part of him. He looks at it now and is suddenly struck by how strange it is—some white guy in a robe, leaning on a cane with a kid on his back. How had he come to attach any importance to a thing like that—a big gold coin, like a piece of foreign currency washed up from the shore of a distant county?

Strange, the way things take on their own meanings.

Chickie sets her glass of milk on the table, watching the way the milk makes little circular waves in the glass, thinking about Bunna, feeling way down deep inside herself the place that still belongs to Bunna, remembering Sister Sarah's prayer: Guard well thy inner door where we reveal our need of Thee.

Chickie will guard Bunna's place forever and ever. If there really is a forever and ever.

Eternity. Father Mullen feels himself on the edge of it, at a deserted beach on the edge of a northern continent watching the ocean rise up into a massive angry swell so large he thinks he may have imagined it, may have imagined everything since one nameless sunny morning in Missouri on the shore of a boyhood pond, long forgotten.

A candle jerks, suddenly, in the Sacred Heart Chapel, snuffing itself out.

Snuffing itself out. That's how Father Flanagan describes it to himself, startled at the thought of a candle, unattended, snuffing itself out in the House of the Lord. He hears, in his mind, a sudden roar so strange, he dismisses it as impossible.

The pipes are rattling, Amiq notices. The pipes always rattle when the little kids sneak down into the basement to swing on them. He remembers when *he* was one of the little ones, daring Sister Sarah to come swat him down.

Saint Christopher, the patron saint of travelers, Amiq thinks, watching the medal swing back and forth on the edge of the rattling metal shelf. *Traveling*, he thinks. His whole life has been about traveling. Traveling away from everything he ever knew—the tundra, the ocean, the sound of the language and the feel of the wind . . .

The pipes complain with a loud crack, and the sink jumps.

"Hey!" Amiq hollers, holding on to the sink. "HEY!"

He imagines those little kids—a whole herd of them—jumping up and swinging from one pipe to the next, yodeling like little Tarzans, then leaping off suddenly into the jungle of the boiler room.

Where the heck was Sister Sarah?

In the cafeteria, a plate rattles violently, and Chickie goes cold with a sudden fear. When the tables and chairs start rattling, too, her muscles freeze. She needs to hold on to something but can't. *Can't move. Can't breathe. Can't breathe.*

The fluorescent bulbs above her tap against each other, and the light flickers ominously. Nausea washes over her.

Sister Mary Kate comes flying out of the kitchen like a white sheet caught in the wind. "Run, Chickie! Run outside!"

The sound of Sister's voice is like a lifeline, pulling her up out of her chair, dragging her away, reminding her muscles to move, move, move. She wants to holler but she can't find her voice. All she can do is stumble behind Sister as though they're connected by an invisible line, Sister, flapping ghost-like in front, plates shattering to the floor behind with a brittle echoing sound.

Earthquake!

Even before he has a chance to name it, every nerve in Luke's body screams the word. Running like crazy down the hall, down the stairs, along corridors, barely aware of all the others bumping and flapping against each other like fish trapped in the bottom of a storm-tossed boat. They are trying to run away from it, only they can't because it's everywhere, even outside.

Even in the sky itself.

Kids and teachers, nuns and priests, all of them outside, running back and forth, trying to decide which way to go, crying and praying and throwing themselves down onto the ground as if onto the back of a giant animal, galloping off into space. Trying to hold on. Everything jerked back and forth like somebody big is playing ball with the planet, somebody as big and mean as Father Mullen's God.

When he looks up to the mountains, Luke feels suddenly dizzy: Even the mountains are rolling back and forth, back and forth. Like huge ships on an angry sea.

Good Friday, Father Mullen thinks. *Good Friday.*

• • •

As the terrible trembling dies down, Chickie realizes, suddenly, that she and Donna are holding hands, clinging to each other's fingers hard enough to crush bones, holding on as if their lives depend on it, neither of them aware of what they're doing.

Their ears fill with a sudden rushing silence that makes Donna feel a terrible loneliness, all of a sudden, like she's standing on God's runway, watching the last plane leave. She feels left behind again, even though she can still feel Chickie's hand. She wants to run after somebody or something. *Don't leave! Don't leave me!*

She lets go of Chickie's hand and sinks to the ground. "Oh." Breathing the word soft as a sigh.

And Chickie knows, feeling Donna's fingers slip from hers, knows suddenly and certainly that there's nothing else to say, nothing left in the whole wide world save the sound of that one word, rising up from Donna's chest like a spirit departed.

Oh.

Their fingers tingle as the blood rushes back into their hands.

Oh.

They both see it at the same time: Sister Sarah, lying on the ground, clutching her chest, motionless.

Luke had watched her fall, fluttering down onto the still-rolling ground, weightless, as if gravity had departed from her skinny old body, her bones at last as light as bird bones.

He'd seen the flickering of her habit, watched Sister Mary Kate fly down beside her, saw Father Flanagan running, running, his robes flapping. And he imagined, for just a second, that the whole world was littered with the black-and-white robes of nuns and priests falling, dropped from the sky like flies or flags.

The ends of his nerves are still jangling with the electricity of it. Even in the center of this sudden stillness, his blood still buzzes.

The sound of things returns, piece by piece, but his head feels stuffed with cotton, noises arriving slowly as if from a great distance: the staccato of scared girls, the squawking of the youngest ones, the sudden shriek of Sister Mary Kate's voice, sharp as gunshot.

"Help! Oh help me! *Please!*"

Sister Mary Kate is kneeling down on the ground next to Sister Sarah, and the pain in Sarah's body is squeezing her face shut tight. Tight as an old fist.

Father Flanagan is still running, his heart pounding in his ears, remembering suddenly just how far they are from everything civilized. Hundreds of miles from the nearest hospital, if there is one left. For a second he even wonders if there really is any help left anywhere.

One of the boys could have carried her alone—it wouldn't take two adults together, but they did it that way anyhow. Sister Sarah and her skinny old body, as hollow as an empty seed husk.

Luke goes cold inside, watching Father and Sister Mary Kate and all the kids, the way they move, everything flowing as if in slow motion. Like he's there but not really there, the same way he felt when they told him the news about Bunna's death, that time.

Sister Sarah is gone. You don't have to look at her to know the truth of it. You can feel it in the air.

It's how the earth decides, he thinks.

They are walking in behind the slow string of nuns and priests and kids, moving cautiously as if afraid to disturb the ground again. Inside, the school looks ravaged, like somebody big ran through all the rooms swinging a two-by-four. Books spilled out of bookcases, windows broken, everything out of place, everyone scurrying everywhere, even into the nuns' quarters. They're so shocked by the sight of it all that nobody thinks about where they're supposed to look or not look.

The strangest thing is Sister Mary Kate's rattail comb, standing upright in a cracked jar of cold cream, right there in the middle of the floor of her room like an alien flower.

In the cafeteria, there's broken glass and spilled food everywhere, but Chickie's glass of milk is still standing on the table, balanced on the very edge as if one sneeze could send it crashing to the floor.

"I'll be darned," Luke says, looking at it. "I'll be doggoned."

Amiq thinks of the Saint Christopher medal, swinging from the edge of a shelf in the empty bathroom, and he wonders whether it fell off into the sink, slid down the drain.

And a thousand miles south, on a remote beach on the southern edge of the northernmost state in the country, Father Mullen watches the ocean rise up over him, a great rushing wall, a ceiling of liquid dark cement raining down. Riveted to the ground, he watches it sweep over him as inevitable as night, watches as though he's watching from a great, unbridgeable distance.

Gone.

It was a heart attack. That's what the whispers say about Sister Sarah, and this seems right somehow, Donna thinks. As though Sister had planned for it in that stern, deliberate way of hers. They bury her at the church graveyard in the woods behind the school. The church was the only family Sister Sarah had, Father says.

Perhaps Sister Sarah had been an orphan, too, just like me, Donna thinks.

They stand in the middle of the graveyard in the woods by the school—a smooth and grassy patch at the tail end of winter. Green things poke up through melting snow, and off through the trees somewhere one little bird tests her song against the crisp air. *Sister Sarah would like it here*, Donna thinks. Then, all of a sudden she knows that Sister *is* here, as much a part of the place as that little hollow of snow and those waving willows. Donna feels her presence as sharp as birdsong, same as always. More real than Father Flanagan's voice, washing over the top of them like water.

Holy Mary, Mother of God. Pray for us sinners now and at the hour of our death.

Luke sees a flash in the woods, and he's pretty sure that nobody else but him sees it. Imagine that: an Eskimo from the treeless tundra knowing enough about the woods to see the old Indian before any of the rest of them see him. But there he is, solid as rock, old Mr. Pete, standing in the cemetery right next to Luke and Chickie.

"What *you* doin' here?" he says to Luke, his voice whispery rough. And for a second Luke is scared, just like the first time. Then he sees the smile. The old, knowing smile, the one that says, "I jokes."

"Sending Sister home," Chickie says.

"She already gone home," the old man says.

Yes, yes she did, Luke thinks, suddenly.

"A heart attack is merciful. A heart attack is so merciful." Sister Mary Kate mutters the words over and over, for days and days, her eyes filling up with tears. Luke feels bad for her because even though she never understood a lot of things, Sister Mary Kate was always good to them. But he can't see how a heart attack is merciful. In fact, he can't see anything at all merciful about death, period. He doesn't even like the sound of the word *mercy*. Tastes like fake sugar, bitter on the tongue.

They say Father Mullen went down to the beach in Seward right before the tidal wave came in. *Tsunami*. This is the word they use. Probably hit him broadside, like a giant two-by-four.

That's what Luke thinks. Swallowed him right up, just like Jonah.

What did Mullen think when he saw that wave coming?

Wrath of God. The words flash through Luke's mind with a sudden rush of sound and sense.

If he were still a kid, he'd want to warn Bunna about Father coming. Tell him to run quick, to get the heck out of there. Now he thinks maybe it's the other way around, maybe old Mullen better watch out for Bunna. But then he realizes that even that's not right. Those two have gone to different places, Bunna and Mullen. Luke knows this as sure as he knows anything.

Bunna's place is with Aapa and Aaka out on the tundra, wide open and golden and full of caribou. Hunting in the sunshine, the way it always shines in the summer at midnight back home. Soft and silent and dreamlike.

In Mullen's place there's a God that gets his energy from punishing people in a heaven so full of the righteous, a person could hardly breathe without pissing someone off. Luke almost laughs out loud: Bunna wouldn't be caught dead in a place like that.

He can't quite explain it about that earthquake, but it's like things were crooked before, and now they're not. Like they weren't lined up, but now they are.

The earth is like that, Luke thinks. *Flipping over and over and over again, trying to right itself, always trying to right itself.*

Epilogue ~ A New Gun
1965

LUKE

The dogs are howling with voices that say a plane is landing, but there's no plane, no distant buzzing in the clouds. It's a new sound making them howl—Uncle Joe's snow machine, come roaring into the yard, bright red and shiny new, the sound of it banging up against our ears like a blizzard against an old shed door.

I like it.

Uncle Joe is kneeling on the seat on one knee, holding hard onto that machine's handles like it's a big animal that needs taming. Isaac sits behind him, grinning hard. His face has grown up, but it's still the same old face, and every time I look at it, it feels like a miracle.

We found him with that ad in the Dallas paper: *Looking for Isaac*. It took a lot of people helping—kids and adults, both. O'Shay's dad did the legal stuff, and Father Flanagan found the money. But we did it. We got him back.

Me and Mom stand at the doorway, watching that snow

machine flash past us, watching its runners carve a wide circle in the snow. The dogs lunge at the ends of their lines, yapping at the edge of that circle like it's a border to a new country, their mouths snapping open and shut with a voiceless violence. It's like a movie with the sound turned off, watching those dogs lunge and snap into the roar of that machine.

The sun against the snow is bright enough to burn your eyes.

"Too much racket!" Mom hollers. "You gonna shake peoples' ears off."

Joe cuts the engine and steps off the machine, never even hearing Mom. He has his gun, his brand-new gun, and he stands in front of that snow machine with that gun strapped across his back like a hunter with a big, shiny catch.

"How you gonna hunt with all that racket?" Mom calls.

Even though it's quiet now, the sound of that machine echoes in our ears, and Mom is yelling like it's still a competition between the two of them.

"Forget the noise!" Isaac hollers back. "It's the speed that counts!"

"This thing goes fast enough you could jump on the back of a running caribou," Joe hollers, then winks at me. "Or rope 'em riding by."

Mom is kneeling down next to Pakak, her lead dog, trying to calm him down, a wisp of gray hair falling across her cheek.

"And what good's all that speed if it can't even find its way home in a storm?" she asks Pakak.

• • •

Isaac's right, though. It's the speed of things going faster and faster in this fast new world—that's what's gonna count, not the noise.

But not right now. Right now, as we sit down to eat, all that matters is us, sitting here at our own table eating frozen fish *quaq* until our stomachs grow warm and our eyes grow sleepy and the world gets slow. All that matters right now is that I'm home and Isaac is finally home, too. And being home is good because I can lean back in my chair and say, "Where's the seal oil?" saying it in Eskimo like I never even left, never even went to Sacred Heart School where they don't know nothing about seal oil, not in any language.

"Where's the *what*?" Uncle Joe says.

I'm slicing off a buttery-smooth slice of frozen fish, suddenly aware of the fact that both Uncle Joe and Mom are looking at me funny, both of them real quiet.

"*Misigaaq*," I say again, the Iñupiaq sounds tickling the back of my throat.

"*Missy-gaq*," Joe says, sliding the jar across the table, mimicking the way I've said it, making me hear how funny it sounds, Catholic-shaped on my Catholic-trained tongue.

"What kind of talk they teach you down there in that place?" Joe asks, laughing. "Swahili?"

And I laugh, too, although there's nothing funny inside my laughter. Inside there's words I can hear, clear as birdsong, words I will never ever say again. Words that make me feel like those dogs out there snapping and lunging, voiceless against the roar of the future.

But never mind, because when the time comes, we're gonna shake everybody's ears off; that's what I think. Shake them good with the sound of all us kids come home, full of new ideas, loud as engines revving. The future may be slick with Latin words and loud machines and the kind of laughter that burns your throat, but it's gonna take off like a shiny new snow machine, ready to go anywhere. Everything, both good and bad, all messed up together. That's what I think.

Uncle Joe is done eating, and he's standing in front of me now, holding his new gun, the gun with the site that's never less than a hair from right. He isn't laughing anymore.

"Guess you're ready for a new gun by now," he says, his voice soft.

Guess I am.

We're roaring across the snow-filled tundra on his snow machine, me and Joe, caribou scattering before us like brown stones rolling across a white run. Joe is focusing on one caribou, a weaker one that's fallen to the side of the herd. As we get closer and closer, we can see the animal's breathing grow labored, see its eye, straining backward, watch how it marks our approach with a look that speaks of resignation. Joe turns his head sideways without taking his eyes off that animal.

"Ready?" He hollers.

I nod my head. I'm ready.

"Hang on!" he yells, raising his body up and leaning out

toward the caribou as we close in on it.

You can see the muscles bunched up on its neck, round as rope. Its nostrils are flared, and its eyes are rolled back, running, always running.

All of a sudden Joe leaps off the machine and lands square on its back, his knife raised. I pull back on the handles and swerve away, the wide-open tundra flying by me like a big white bird. I take one long icy breath and smile.

It tastes like life, that breath.

Author's Note

My Name Is Not Easy is a work of fiction, but the story of Sacred Heart School and its students is based on a number of real places and real events in Alaska history. Prior to the Molly Hootch settlement of 1976, which required the State of Alaska to fund schools in even the smallest and most remote Alaskan villages, there were virtually no high schools in the vast region known as "bush" Alaska. To earn a diploma, children from the Bush were forced to travel hundreds and sometimes thousands of miles from their homes to live at distant boarding schools for months or years at a time. Many were sent away at very young ages. Virtually all of these students were Native Alaskans, and most attended schools operated by the Bureau of Indian Affairs, such as Mount Edgecumbe in Sitka, Alaska, and Wrangell Institute on Wrangell Island. Some traveled as far as Chemawa, in Oregon, and Chilocco, in Oklahoma. And some attended Copper Valley, a parochial boarding school located in the vast central portion of Alaska known as the Interior, a school that educated both Native and non-Native students. *My Name Is Not Easy* is based on the many stories I have heard from the alumni of these schools, most of whom are my contemporaries, close friends, and relatives.

Many of the events in *My Name Is Not Easy* actually did happen. Students at the Copper Valley School did earn a bus with Betty Crocker coupons, and they did earn tuition by hunting and were, unbelievably, allowed to keep their guns in their rooms. Junior is a fictional character, but his "uncle" Howard Rock—the editor of *Tundra Times*—was a real person, originally from the village of Point Hope, just a few miles north of the very real proposed site of Project Chariot. Project Chariot was conceived by the Atomic Energy Commission as a means of demonstrating the peaceful use of atomic energy by creating a new ocean harbor through a series of simultaneous nuclear blasts 189 times the size of the one that leveled the Japanese city of Hiroshima.

The Barrow Duck-In is also a real historical event. The Duck-In and Project Chariot are the topics of two documentary films written and directed by my daughter, the filmmaker Rachel Edwardson, and produced by Jana Harcharek, director of Inupiat Education for the North Slope Borough School District.

The military's Cold Weather Research iodine-131 experiments were conducted in the late 1950s in the Iñupiaq villages of Wainwright, Point Lay, Point Hope, and Anaktuvik Pass, and in the Athabascan villages of Fort Yukon and Arctic Village—as well as at Copper Valley School. Researchers wanted to find out why Native peoples living above the Arctic Circle seemed to thrive in cold weather, while non-Natives suffered. They wondered whether the thyroid gland played a role in regulating the body's ability to withstand extreme cold, but later found out that it does not. In 2000, following the release of a study done by the National Research Council, the North Slope Borough obtained a settlement for the victims of iodine-131 testing who had lived in the villages under its jurisdiction. Although the National Research Council has concluded that those tested as children were at the highest risk of developing cancer, none of those who were tested as boarding-school students have received settlements or acknowledgement of any sort. Some of these people have since died of cancer.

The Good Friday earthquake of 1964, measuring 9.2 on the Richter Scale, was the largest earthquake ever to hit North America and the second-largest earthquake ever recorded. This earthquake caused 115 deaths in Alaska, 106 of which were due to tsunamis.

The story of Luke, Bunna, and Isaac is based, in part, on the story of three real brothers. Those brothers did have an uncle who told them that Catholics eat horse meat. The middle brother did die in a plane crash, flying home from boarding school. The older brother was not on that plane because he did, in fact, have a premonition about it and did try to stop his brother from flying. The youngest brother was adopted out, without the family's permission. He grew up in Texas and returned home as an adult.

I know these stories well because I married the oldest brother. His real name is George Edwardson. I never knew my brother-in-law Bunna, and for reasons I still do not fully understand, I was unable to change his name, despite the fact that his story, as recorded here, is indeed fiction.

Most of the older leaders of Native Alaska today were, like

my husband, educated at boarding schools. The "family" network that boarding-school students created among themselves still survives today and has been instrumental in affecting the many political changes that marked twentieth-century history in Native Alaska. Students similar to the students of Sacred Heart became leaders in their home communities—state legislators, city mayors, and tribal presidents. These people lobbied for change in Washington, D.C., and united their tribes to speak forcefully with one voice through the Alaska Federation of Natives, the organization that was instrumental in securing passage of the Alaska Native Claims Settlement Act (ANCSA).

ANCSA returned 40 million acres of Alaskan land to Native ownership, paying a cash settlement of $900 billion to compensate for lands lost. The land and money was distributed through a network of regional and village corporations. Most of those who organized and ran ANCSA corporations were once boarding-school students.

I wrote *My Name Is Not Easy* for the children and grandchildren of these people—my own included—to let them know what their relatives endured, so they can look not only at what they lost but, of equal importance, at what they learned and how they used it.

Acknowledgments

As always, I am eternally grateful to my mentors at Vermont College of the Fine Arts: the brilliant Louise Hawes; the inimitable and endlessly intuitive Tim Wynne-Jones; Ellen Levine, an indefatigable supporter who never, for one moment, doubted me (and who said once that hefting around the massive initial manuscript was increasing her upper body strength); and Marion Dane Bauer, whose wisdom and passionate belief in this story have meant everything to me. Thank you, too, to my daughter Rachel Edwardson, whose research on the Duck-In and Project Chariot fed this story; and to the staff of Tuzzy Library in Barrow, Alaska: David Ongley, Sara Saxton, and Gabe Tegoseak, who researched the obscure, forgave overdue notices, fixed obsolete microfiche readers, and generally indulged me.